EXIT

A NOVEL BY

FRANKIE BERRY WISE

WISE Scholars Publishing

"We Bring Life **to** Learning"

First published by WISE Scholars Publishing, August 2012
(Second Edition published, June 2016)

Atlanta, Georgia USA 30318

10 9 8 7 6 5 4 3 2 1

www.wisescholarspublishing.com

Library of Congress Cataloging-in-Publication Data

Wise, Frankie Berry
Exit

Summary: *Exit* is a fictional mystery. The story revolves around the character Lee, who was recently contacted by her first love to secretly meet in their hometown of Alabaster, Georgia. Lee is hesitant because not only is she happily married, but also her lost love has abandoned her in the past.

Since Lee's first love only reappears when it is convenient for him, will Lee run to be by his side again? Or will she resist the urge and stay faithful to her loyal husband? Who will Lee choose? The man that she has always loved or the man that she exchanged vows with?

While contemplating which decision to make, Lee encounters an odd character by the name of Sister. Trying to persuade Lee to avoid traveling back down the same road as before, Sister shares the story of another character named Pookie McAdoo.

What does Pookie's story have to do with Lee? How do the lives of Sister, Pookie, and Lee intertwine within this heart-wrenching mystery?

Paperback:
ISBN-13: 9781478373889
ISBN-10: 1478373881 1

Hardback:
ISBN-13: 978-0-9963946-2-8
ISBN-10: 0-9963946-2-1
Printed in the United States of America

Cover design: Soweto Bosia, Blue Boy Media
Copy Editing: Dr. N. Jeff Carden, III
Substantive Editing: Marshalette R. Wise, WISE Scholars Publishing

DEDICATION

This book is dedicated to my husband, Garland, and our five children: Monica, Michele, Michael, Marcos, and Marshalette.

CHAPTER 1

Lee opened her eyes and yawned. She pulled her crème silk sheets tightly over her body after pushing her black duvet to the side. She would have liked to lounge in bed most of the morning, drinking chamomile tea or staring at the tropical fish as they swam back and forth in her saltwater aquarium. However, she would have to enjoy the comforts of her bedroom another day.

On this particular morning, she wanted to cook her husband, Sam, a special breakfast before he departed for his trip overseas. He and his band would be embarking on a two-month European musical tour.

As Lee sat up against several plush pillows, she glanced at the clock on her bedside table. Realizing that she had overslept, she quickly threw on her satin robe and furry slippers before rushing downstairs.

She was extremely disappointed to learn that her maid, Mrs. Mabel Hemphill, had already prepared Sam's breakfast. As she peered out of the large glass door leading to one of their balconies, she barely caught the tail end of their red antique truck as he was leaving the driveway.

Although Lee wanted to see Sam before his trip, she was somewhat relieved that she had not. That was largely due to the fact that she was keeping a secret from him that, if discovered, could possibly end their marriage.

After returning to her bedroom, she opened her nightstand drawer and removed a letter that she had hidden. It was from her first love and lover, a famous singer who had once headlined some of the biggest concerts and tours. He had recently sent the letter through Lee's publicist, requesting that she secretly meet him in the same town where, many years ago, they initially had crossed paths.

Lee had advised her publicist to let him know that she would indeed meet him. He claimed that he would be eagerly awaiting her arrival and if she did not show, he would never bother her again.

As Lee held his letter, rereading it as she sat on the edge of her ottoman, she reminisced about the love they had once shared. However, her desire and eagerness to reconnect with him was suddenly overshadowed by bitterness and fear. So many times, in the past, she had needed him both emotionally and physically, but he would always conveniently disappear at her most vulnerable times. Now that she was a semi-successful singer—married to an equally established recording artist—her lost love had suddenly reappeared, seeking her to be at his beck and call. But what about her husband, Sam, who had always been there when she needed him? Did he deserve such betrayal? Was getting closure worth jeopardizing her marriage?

Sam had been faithful to Lee ever since she first met him. He comforted her after the death of her brother, mother, and stepfather. Sam even encouraged Lee to vigorously pursue her singing career, giving her the motivation not to abandon her dream of making it to the big time. He also helped to keep her grounded, persuading her to live in Ohio in lieu of the flashy lights and facade of Beverly Hills. Because of Sam's successful career, Lee was even able to take a much-needed break from show business to focus just on being his wife.

Nevertheless, Lee could not escape the insatiable desire to see her first love, face-to-face, one more time. Sure, she could pick up any gossip magazine from a supermarket, and read all the rumors about the women he had dated, the mansions that he had purchased, or the luxury sports cars he drove. But, Lee knew him before his fame. It was the small-town, country boy in him that made her fall in love. Although never reaching the height of his celebrity status—Lee knew all too well how the music business could bring fake friends, with ulterior motives, into your life. What she and he had shared was real, or so she would have liked to think. But was it possible to love two men at the same time? Or was one of them true love and the other mere convenience?

As Lee put the letter back into its hiding place, her eyes were drawn to the small frame on the top of the nightstand. The frame held an old photo of her mother. She suddenly remembered one of her mother's words of advice: "Your past stays on your ass; be sure your ass has the room to carry it."

Lee picked up the small picture and stared into her mother's face, envisioning she was still alive to help her sort out the tangled web she had weaved. As she pondered her mother's advice, she heard Mabel humming as she dusted Sam's office.

Mabel and her husband, Jed, had been working for Lee and Sam for many years. Although Mabel was only a few years older, she considered her like a second mother. Lee decided to ask her for some much needed advice. She gently set the picture back on the nightstand before walking across the hall to Sam's office.

"Mabel," Lee called.

"I'm in here, Mrs. Lee," Mabel replied as she polished Sam's mahogany desk. "I didn't see you standing there."

"I'm sorry… I didn't mean to startle you."

"If you're looking for Mr. Sam… Jed drove him to the airport about forty minutes ago."

"I know. I saw them as they drove away."

"Mr. Sam didn't want to disturb you."

"That was considerate of him. I overslept as usual."

"I prepared his breakfast and left yours on the kitchen counter."

"Thanks, Mabel."

"You're most welcome, Mrs. Lee."

"I'll be in my room if you need me," Lee said, turning to go before hesitating.

"Mrs. Lee, is there something you want to ask me?"

"Yes, Mabel… there is."

Leaving the oily cloth on top of the desk, Mabel pulled her shoulder-length salt and pepper hair away from her chocolate face. She then sat down in Sam's leather chair, giving Lee her undivided attention.

"Well... has a male lover, from your past, ever asked you to see him just one more time?" Lee asked, getting directly to the point before she changed her mind.

"Once, but I kept putting it off until it was too late," Mabel responded, with no hesitation.

"What happened?"

"He eventually died before we could meet again."

"I'm sorry to hear that, Mabel."

"That's life. If you don't make the decision, death will."

"So true," Lee said, softly.

Mabel left the comfort of Sam's chair and walked over to the window. She stared out into the backyard, where she noticed that Jed had returned from driving Sam to the airport. He was on his knees, pulling weeds out of the rose garden.

"Sometimes, I wonder did I make the right choice," Mabel said in a somber voice. "Or was the choice made for me? I guess I'll never know the answer to those questions."

Lee went to the window and stood beside Mabel. They both watched the unassuming Jed, who rarely smiled or held a conversation with anyone, except Sam. When he did smile, his mouth turned into a thin line under his nose. Lee could not remember Jed ever wearing anything but overalls.

"Now… if I may be so bold… when are we going to see a little Lee or Sam running around this huge house?" Mabel asked, as they continued to watch Mr. Jed.

"Sam and I are doing our best," Lee lied, blushing as she rubbed her flat stomach. "We put off having children to pursue our musical careers."

Lee felt guilty lying to Mabel. She knew in her heart that she was not doing her best to conceive. In fact, against Sam's knowledge, she was taking great precautions not to get pregnant. This was due to certain things in her past that made her fearful to embrace her maternal instinct to procreate.

"Why didn't you and Mr. Jed have any children?"

"Jed said that fatherhood wasn't for him. When I asked him why, he never gave me an answer. So, we just remained childless."

"Sometimes the answer lies in our past," Lee said

in a whisper.

"What did you say?"

"Nothing," Lee answered quickly.

Lee had suddenly made her decision; there would be no more pondering. She decided emphatically that she would take that journey to see her old boyfriend. Lee's decision was motivated primarily by two considerations. Firstly, she wanted to discover if their old flames still burned for one another and, secondly, to prove to him that she was no longer the shy, young girl that he used to know.

"I've decided to travel down south for a few days. Would you and Mr. Jed take care of the house while I'm gone?"

"Don't worry; we always do."

"I knew that I could depend on you."

"When will you be leaving?"

"Early tomorrow morning."

"Do you want me to help you pack?"

"No, thanks. I can manage it myself."

"Do you have your house keys?"

"Right here," Mabel said, jingling them in her pocket.

"Thanks again, Mabel. I'll be in my room."

"Are you sure you don't need any help?"

"No, Mabel. As a matter of fact… you and Mr. Jed can take the rest of the day off."

"Thanks, Mrs. Lee. I'll let Jed know that we can leave early."

"That'll be just fine. I'll see y'all when I get back from my trip."

Lee returned to her bedroom, excited and filled with anticipation. She was looking forward to beginning her journey on tomorrow morning.

She thought, "It's going to be nice to drive the nearly six-hundred miles down south to Alabama from Cincinnati. The leaves on the trees will be green and the roadsides will be covered with the blooms of black-eyed Susan's and wild dogwood trees. There'll be fields of planted cotton, corn, and watermelon. Beautiful antebellum homes, with cows and horses roaming on farmlands, will be a joy to see. I'll stay a night at one of those small-town hotels and eat dinner in one of those country diners."

Her thoughts were momentarily interrupted by the sounds of the front door closing and then Mabel and Jed backing out of the driveway.

As she began to pack her luggage, she felt dizzy and unsteady. She held onto the bedpost until her head stopped spinning and she was confident that she would not fall.

Lee thought that it was probably because she had not eaten, and it was far past breakfast. She reasoned that since she was diabetic, her blood sugar must have dropped. So she decided that she would quickly finish packing and then go downstairs to eat the food that Mabel had prepared.

The rows of clothes and shelves of shoes in her walk-in closet were overwhelming. She suddenly wished she had accepted Mabel's help, but it was too late.

Finally, Lee mustered up enough energy to finish sorting her belongings. However, her bedroom was now in a shamble. The dresser drawers hung open, clothes were strewn across the chaise lounge, and shoes covered the Persian rug. Lee hated to leave her bedroom so untidy, but she was certain that Mabel would have it in order by the time she returned.

Lee attempted to walk downstairs, but felt too unsteady. She was faintish and her hands trembled uncontrollably. She laid across the bed, on her stomach, searching the bedside table for something to boost her energy. She found a piece of candy in the bottom drawer. Lee quickly ate it before instantly dosing off to sleep.

The sun shining brightly through her bedroom window awakened Lee. She could hear the birds chirping as butterflies and bumblebees fed from honeysuckles and morning glory vines, growing near the pond behind her house. She was surprised to learn that she had slept throughout the evening and into the next morning. Although still somewhat dizzy, she was eager to begin her journey.

Lee took great precautions getting off the bed, carefully placing her feet on the floor. She then heard the telephone ringing. Hoping that it was Sam, Lee hurried to answer it. To her delight, it was indeed his voice on the other end.

Sam informed her that he and his band had arrived safely to Europe. He also told her that he loved her and that he was looking forward to her joining him in three weeks.

When Sam inquired about her plans for the weekend, Lee did not tell him about her trip to Alabama. Instead she claimed that she would be spending time with some girlfriends, shopping, dining, and going to the spa.

After hanging up the telephone, Lee got dressed in a pair of blue jeans, a white shirt, and tennis shoes. She dragged her two designer suitcases to the top of the stairs, pushing each piece down the steps.

With her luggage in the trunk, the top down on her convertible Mercedes Benz, and a tank full of gasoline, Lee began her drive down south.

Would seeing her old lover offer the closure she needed? Perhaps this was just another chapter in a twisted saga of what could, should, or might have been? Was it simply a dream? Or maybe, it was merely a nightmare?

(TO BE CONTINUED)

CHAPTER 2

Lee had been driving for hours when she finally saw the sign, Welcome to Georgia - Wisdom, Justice, Moderation. In her peripheral vision, she spotted what appeared to be a dirty and disheveled person, walking on the side of the road.

Lee believed the person—wearing a faded blue cap, white t-shirt, a pair of torn jeans, and worn-out tennis shoes—was a boy. That was until she had driven past and realized the person was a young girl.

She thought to herself, "She reminds me of myself when I was younger. Where in the world could she be going?"

Lee wanted to stop and offer the girl a ride, but she had promised Sam that she would never give a ride to a stranger.

Exhausted from the long drive, Lee searched for a place to pull over and rest. She drove approximately a mile farther down the highway before taking the next EXIT. She immediately saw a sign that read, Wilma's Diner & Inn – The Best Food & Sleep in Town. Lee reasoned that instead of pulling off to the side of the road that she might as well eat and possibly spend the night there.

She mumbled, "The last thing I need is for someone to run a salacious story with the headline, 'Has-been star caught sleeping on the side of the road… Was she drunk or high on drugs?'" Besides unwanted publicity, the last thing Lee needed was for any rumors to trickle down to her husband, Sam.

She parked next to the only other car in the diner's parking lot. Lee got out of her car and walked to the door, opening it and going inside. There were only two customers: a woman with ash-blonde hair and a man seated at a different table. Lee sat in a booth next to the nearest window.

An obese woman, carrying a large bowl of cornflakes, came out of the kitchen. She had kinky, graying hair and her apron was covered with stains. She took the bowl of cereal over to the man's table and set it in front of the man. She then handed him a spoon that she cleaned with her dirty apron. The man began to quickly eat the cereal, dripping milk down his chin and onto his red plaid shirt.

The woman with the ash-blonde hair stared, glassy-eyed, at the man as he sopped up the cereal. Her watery eyes appeared to be a mixture of those of a person who had been crying all night and one who had not gotten enough sleep. Her face was extremely wrinkled and aged beyond her years. It was obvious that she had lived a hard life. With trembling hands, she chain-smoked cigarettes from one of the three packs that set in front of her. One after another—she lit, puffed, deeply swallowed, and then simultaneously exhaled through her nose and mouth. She constantly licked her chapped, tobacco-stained lips in between smoking. Having already filled her ashtray with butts, she had begun to flick her ashes into her plate of country-fried steak and mash potatoes.

"Welcome to Wilma's Diner," the obese woman said, handing Lee a food-stained menu. "The apple pie is delicious; I made it myself."

"A cup of coffee, please," Lee responded, taking the menu and setting it to the side. The appearance of the two customers, coupled with the obese waitress, had spoiled her appetite.

"This must be your first time," the woman said.

"Yes, it is."

"Hey… you look familiar."

"Do I? I've been told I have that type of face."

"Yeah… you look like that blues singer… What's

her name? Ahhh… I forget now. But, she was very popular. Gossip is that she has become a recluse and is hardly seen in Hollywood circles anymore."

"I don't read the gossip magazines much," Lee retorted, not revealing that she was, in fact, the singer that the waitress spoke of. "I'm just passing through."

"We all are."

"Excuse me," Lee replied, unsure of what the woman was implying.

"I'm Wilma," the woman said, ignoring Lee's comment.

"Glad to meet you, Wilma."

"Be right back with your coffee," Wilma said, returning to the kitchen.

Lee continued to observe the man and woman while she waited for her coffee. She then heard the diner door opening. Looking in the direction of the sound, Lee was surprised to see that it was the young girl that she had seen walking.

As Wilma returned with Lee's coffee and a slice of pie, the girl removed her backpack and clutched it tightly. Dirty and sweaty, she remained standing as if she was contemplating fleeing.

"I only ordered coffee," Lee said.

"The pie is free," Wilma responded, setting the coffee and pie on the table. "I greet all of my new customers with a slice of my homemade, apple pie."

"Thanks," Lee said, while noticing the juicy apples falling from the golden-brown crust.

"You're welcome," Wilma replied, quickly turning her attention toward the young girl. "I'll be right with you. You can sit anywhere you like."

"I just want a glass of water," a girlish voice retorted, not moving from where she stood.

"A glass of water isn't enough for a growing teen. I'll bring you a slice of my apple pie."

"I don't have enough money."

"Bless your heart, darling. You just have a seat and I'll be right back."

"Thank you," the girl responded as she scanned the diner for a booth.

As the waitress turned to go to the kitchen, Lee called out to her. "Wilma, I changed my mind. Bring me two plates of your dinner specials… one for me and one for her."

"Coming right up," Wilma responded.

Lee motioned for the girl to join her. Apprehensively, the girl sat at Lee's booth while still tightly gripping her backpack.

"My name is Lee. What's your name?"

"People call me Sister."

"Well, Sister… you're welcome to share my food. I ordered plenty."

Relaxing the grip on her backpack, Sister finally set it on the side of her. She removed her blue cap and placed it on her lap, exposing her short, black curly hair. Her brown eyes were expressionless and sunken deep into her pale face. Lee could not help but notice that her bosom was as flat as a boy's chest.

"Thanks for sharing your food with me," Sister said shyly.

"You're welcome. I saw you walking some miles back. I wanted to give you a ride, but the traffic was too heavy for me to stop."

"There's always other rides to take you where you think you want to go," Sister responded with a stoic look on her face.

The woman with the ash-blonde hair collected her last pack of cigarettes and put it in an old, green purse. She wobbled, in run-down shoes, over to where the man was sitting. Sunlight from the windows shone through her dingy dress, exposing her bony legs. Lee realized that the man and woman must have been together and were just sitting separately when the woman wiped milk off of his shirt and chin. She then helped him to stand up before guiding him towards the door.

"Wilma... me and my old man is leaving," the woman said, taking a pair of sunglasses from her purse and putting them over the man's eyes. "We'll see you tomorrow."

"I'll be here," Wilma responded.

On a large tray, Wilma brought two plates of food over to where Lee and Sister were sitting. Sister began to eat as soon as Wilma set the plates of fried chicken, mashed potatoes with gravy, string beans, and cornbread down. In between chewing, she took audible gulps from the pint-sized jar of tea.

"Eat as much as you want," Lee said before turning towards Wilma. "Who was that man and woman?"

"That was Mary Youngblood and her blind husband, John," Wilma answered. "They've been coming here for a long time."

"Why do they seem so…."

"Desolate," Wilma said, finishing Lee's question.

"That's exactly the word I was searching for."

"If you want to know… you'll have to ask them," Wilma said.

"It's the road chosen," Sister interrupted through a food-filled mouth.

"What do you mean, Sister?" Lee asked, puzzled.

"If you change roads, you get lost," Sister replied. "No matter how hard you try, you can't find your way back to where you began."

"I'll be in the kitchen," Wilma said, leaving them alone.

"Sister," Lee asked, "how far is your journey taking you?"

"Back to where I began. How far are you going?"

"I'm going to Alabaster, Georgia. It's about two hundred miles from here."

"I was there once many years ago. I kept telling myself to go back one more time and everything will correct itself, but it never did. I had become like a compulsive gambler, trying unsuccessfully to win back all of the money I had lost," Sister said, looking at the EXIT sign over the diner's door.

"You were in Alabaster before?" Lee asked, surmising that Sister was embellishing her story as she talked.

"When I walk out that door, I'm turning around and going back."

"Going back where?" Lee asked, nonplused.

"Back to where I came from."

"Then why did you come this far just to turn around?"

"To find the courage to turn back... to stop walking over the same old skeletons that I left behind so many years ago. The bones have now become dry and brittle. For some reason, no matter how hard I try, they continue to crumble under my feet." Sister then looked directly into Lee's eyes and said, "If I were you, I would go back before it's too late."

Lee had had enough of Sister's morbid predictions. She assured herself, "Nothing is going to happen on my trip that I can't handle. Besides, Sister seems like she is some kind of whacked out teenager, whose brainwaves had been destroyed by drugs."

Lee forced herself to take a bite of Wilma's food. Surprisingly, it was very delicious. She and Sister devoured every morsel, including the apple pie. As they sat silently, with full stomachs, Wilma emerged from the kitchen.

"There's a storm coming," Wilma declared, wiping her hands on her apron. "I'm closing the diner, locking the door, and hiding under one of these tables."

"It doesn't seem stormy to me," Lee replied, looking out of the window at a clear blue sky. She believed that Wilma was also somewhat mentally unhinged.

"What are you two going to do?" Wilma asked. "Are y'all staying until the storm is over?"

"Thanks Wilma, but I'm going to continue on," Lee answered. "What about you, Sister?"

“I’m leaving,” Sister replied. “I’m going back the way I came.”

“Child… a storm is coming,” Wilma repeated. “You might as well stay here for a night or two. You can eat in the diner and sleep upstairs.”

“I don’t need any charity!” Sister retorted.

“I’ve never donated to a charity in my life,” Wilma said, winking one eye at Lee. “You can pay your debt by helping me in the kitchen.”

“When I return in a few days, you can ride back the way you came with me,” Lee offered.

“You better stay here, too, until the storm has passed,” Wilma advised Lee.

“Sorry, Wilma… but I’m on a schedule,” Lee said apologetically. “I must be going.”

“Well… if you say so.”

“How much do I owe you for the food?” Lee asked, trying to hand her two crisp hundred-dollar bills.

“You can pay me when you return,” Wilma said, refusing the money. “And I promise you… you WILL return!”

Unbeknownst to Wilma, Lee slid the money into the pocket of her apron as she cleared their plates from the table.

Lee waved goodbye to Sister and Wilma as she walked out of the diner. She closed the door and momentarily held onto the handle, flabbergasted by all that had transpired. Through the window, she could see them gathering candles. They were placing one on every booth in the event the electricity went off.

Lee was, more so than before, confident that Wilma was a mad woman. She did not see any signs of an approaching storm. Neither was there a cloud in the sky. However, in the event Wilma was correct, Lee closed the top of her convertible before driving away.

As she approached the main highway, she found it peculiar that she was the only car on the road. She continued to drive, hoping she was going in the right direction.

The weather seemed unusually hot. Even with the air conditioner blowing against her face, Lee was perspiring profusely. She finally began to cool down and relax after seeing two large yellow signs, one pointing toward Alabaster and the other toward an EXIT.

However, her relaxation did not last long. In a matter of seconds, the weather drastically changed. The bright, sunlit sky turned dark and cloudy. Lightning flashed as thunder roared. Strong winds began to rock her car back and forth while heavy rain blinded her view. Lee quickly turned on the hazard lights and wipers, driving with her face close to the steering wheel. If it were not for the flashes of lightning, the road would have been completely obscured. Lee thought, "Wilma was right. It's too dangerous to be out here. I must make it back to the diner." She then took the road pointing toward the EXIT in order to turn around in lieu of continuing onward.

Eventually, Lee made it back to the candlelit diner. Sighing with relief, she rumbled through the backseat, looking for an umbrella. She then remembered that it was in the trunk.

Lee decided to wait a few minutes in hopes that the rain would subside. Furthermore, she was in no mood to hear Wilma say, "I told you so." Nevertheless, as the storm worsened, Lee decided it was time to swallow her pride and hurry into the diner.

She opened the car door, but quickly closed it when she saw headlights approaching. Two cars, both parking on each side of her, came to a sudden stop and turned off their lights. Shadowy images of frantic people scrambled from their cars, hurrying to the diner and disappearing inside.

Realizing the worst of the storm was yet to come, Lee decided to follow suit. Against the strong wind, she forced the door open. She was barely able to reclose it. Lee struggled to run to the entrance of the diner, trying to maintain her footing against the ferocious wind. The rain was pouring down as debris was flying about.

Ironically, the door to the diner was locked. She began to bang against it, hoping someone would hear her. Lee could not comprehend how the last group of people was able to simply run inside without issue, yet she was trapped outside.

A very tall man, neatly dressed in a gray suit and tie, finally opened the door. After Lee walked into the dimly lit diner, he shut the door behind her and abruptly walked away. With both hands, she wiped rainwater from her face. Water, dripping from her wet clothes, caused a puddle to form on the floor.

Oddly, the man that had opened the door for Lee began to march around in a circle. Mumbling incoherently to himself, he went from looking like a businessman to a lunatic.

Two men and three women, sitting at a table in a dark corner, were chatting among themselves. A little boy and girl, dressed in white clothing, ran and played in the empty booths.

Wilma, carrying a large tray of food, emerged from the kitchen. With a towel across her left shoulder, she placed the food in front of the two men and three women.

Lee was expecting for Wilma to offer her the towel, but she instead took the money that Lee had secretly given her and insisted that she take it back.

"I told you to pay me when you return from your journey!"

"I've decided to take another route home."

"But, there isn't another route. This is the only way back."

Lee sighed at Wilma's foolishness, seeing no reason to get into a debate. Her main objective was to wait until the storm was over so she could get far away from all of the weird people in the diner.

She then went to search for Sister. Lee eventually found her, sitting on the floor in a corner.

Upon noticing Lee, Sister took a book out of her backpack, opened it, and began to read. The glistening candles in front of Sister, coupled with the sudden standoffish behavior of Wilma, reminded Lee of something out of the twilight zone. She contemplated pinching herself in order to ensure that she was not, in fact, dreaming.

"Sister," Lee called, waiting for a response. "I had to return to the diner because Wilma was right about the storm. I'm going to wait here until it passes and then I'll continue on my journey."

Sister slowly raised her head, momentarily glancing at Lee, before continuing to read.

"Sister… did you hear what I said?" Lee asked, feeling shunned and confused.

Realizing that Sister was intentionally ignoring her, Lee left her to her solitude and went to talk with Wilma, who was cleaning the floor with a moldy-smelling mop.

"Wilma… you were right about the storm," Lee conceded, swallowing her pride.

"I know," Wilma responded, leaning the mop against the wall. "Were you glad to see your friends?"

"What friends?"

"Your friends in the diner," Wilma replied, agitated as though Lee's question was invalid.

"I don't know any of these people," Lee said, growing equally irritated. "Except for you and Sister, they're all strangers to me!"

"They're not strangers! They're your folks and mine! They're the relatives we've left behind and the relatives that went before us."

"If you say so," Lee said, attempting to appease her.

Lee's attention was then drawn to the sounds of arguing coming from the customers. They were talking loudly, deciding whether to turn back or to continue on their journey once the storm abated.

The children, who had been joyfully playing, were now crying. And the man, in the gray suit, was still pacing.

Sister, who had been sitting on the floor, walked to and stood in the middle of the diner. With the book in her hand, she began to read aloud. Wilma, leaving Lee at the door, went to join her.

The customers abruptly stopped bickering and stared at Sister and Wilma. The expressionless man stopped circling and sat on the floor with his legs tucked underneath him. His mannerisms were as if he had the mind of a five-year old child. Suddenly, the children stopped crying and sat attentively in a booth across from the adults.

Lee began to fear the diner's occupants more than the worsening storm. Feeling trapped, she astutely tried to assess the situation.

With everyone's undivided attention—Sister continued to read aloud from the book, starting from the beginning.

"Sister… I'll be leaving when the storm is over," Lee interrupted, pretending as though she was not fearful of the diner's occupants. Continuing her façade, she insincerely asked, "Do you want me to give you a ride somewhere?"

"I've been to the same place you're going many times," Sister responded, answering Lee's question without taking her eyes away from the book. "Nothing is there for me or you, but the past."

Lee mumbled under her breath, "I need to get the hell away from these crazy people!" She then decided to take her chances and wait out the rest of the storm in her car. She briskly walked toward the EXIT. However before she could reach to open the door, the man that was wearing the gray suit sat against it, preventing her from leaving.

As Lee's fight-or-flight response was about to be triggered, Sister called out to her in desperation.

"Please don't leave until I finish reading my story," Sister begged.

"Come… let's take a seat," Wilma added, taking Lee by the hand. "The storm will be over soon and you can be on your way."

"What's the title of your book?" Lee asked. "I'll buy a copy and read it later."

"It doesn't have a title," Sister replied. "If you stay… I'll travel down that road with you when the storm is over… regardless of which direction you choose to go."

Feeling helpless, Lee agreed and sat in a booth next to Wilma. She briefly thought about Sam, wondering how his European tour was going. Lee then envisioned her lost love, waiting with open arms for her arrival.

"Maybe, you can help give her story a name," Wilma whispered in Lee's ear, breaking her train of thought and refocusing them on Sister.

As the storm raged outside, there was not a sound from anyone inside. The only voice that could be heard was Sister's as she read her story from the beginning for the final time.

CHAPTER 3

The laxative Pookie had taken the night before kept her confined to the small bathroom. She amused herself by looking out of the window at her mother, Shug, and her brother, June Bug, as they picked up trash from the yard. Shug was putting the trash into a garbage bag while June Bug held it open.

Pookie tried to do chores around the house. However, the laxative would soon send her hurrying to sit over the pee-stained commode. Her dingy, once white, panties dangled just above her knees.

After she finished, she cleaned her buttocks with the last of the toilet tissue. She dropped the fecal covered tissue into the commode and flushed it. The sewage line, clogged with mounds of paper and tree roots, expelled Pookie's mess. Suddenly, the dirty toilet water began to rise to the top of the commode. She quickly jumped to her feet and watched the mess finally sink out of sight before pulling up her panties around her waist.

She then stood at the small window, watching her mother and brother work in the yard. As June Bug pulled his red wagon, Shug took bags of trash and set them by the curb.

But this time, Shug and June Bug were not alone. On this Wednesday, instead of Johnny Overtree driving into the driveway and tooting the horn for Shug to come outdoors to retrieve the basket of clothes that Mr. and Mrs. Bill Roberson wanted her to iron—he decided to linger longer than usual.

Driving Mr. Bill's red truck and wearing a blue cap with "Bill's Hardware" written across the front, Johnny parked in the yard and carried the basket of wrinkled clothes towards the door. When Pookie looked out, she saw Shug and him, talking as they walked toward the house.

Pookie quickly moved away from the window when she heard the front door open. She wanted to escape to her bedroom, but it was too late. Johnny and Shug had come inside of the house. Embarrassed and hidden in a bathtub filled with dirty clothes, Pookie decided to remain in the smelly, hot bathroom until Johnny left. From her hiding place, she could hear him and Shug's conversation. Pookie could not believe that Johnny Overtree, the man she secretly loved, was in her home.

She could hear Johnny, following Shug down the hallway toward June Bug's bedroom. Shug carried the clothesbasket into her son's room where the iron and ironing board were always ready for use. She placed the basket on top of June Bug's bed. Johnny did not follow Shug into the bedroom. Instead, he sat on the floor in the hallway and rested his back against the stained wall as he listened to Shug, chattering about how the Roberson's do not pay her enough to iron their clothes and clean their house.

Shug plugged the iron's frayed cord into the exposed socket and waited for it to heat. She talked continuously to Johnny until he finally interrupted her.

"I should be on my way back to the store," Johnny said abruptly. "What do you want me to tell Mr. Bill? Do you want Pookie to take that evening job at his store?"

"We could use the extra money," Shug said, looking up at the rain-spotted ceiling. "Tell Mr. Bill that Pookie will take that job. With the extra money, maybe we could move to a better house and neighborhood. I'm sick of living in this rat and crime-infested neighborhood."

"I know how it must feel Miss Shug."

"Maybe Pookie could return to high school and graduate," Shug replied, wishfully thinking. "I should take my children and do what Ruby did."

"What did Mrs. Ruby do?"

"Ruby left this godforsaken neighborhood," Shug said in a high-pitched voice. "She didn't tell her best friend, Tilly, or me! She just disappeared!"

"Where's June Bug?" Johnny asked, interrupting Shug's story.

"Pookie," Shug shouted, "check on your brother! Hurry up before he wonders off and gets lost!" As she placed a shirt on the ironing board and grabbed the iron, she added, "And don't forget to hang the wet clothes on the lines. Let June Bug help you!"

Shug and Pookie had made it their policy to never let June Bug out of their sight. He had a habit of removing all of his clothes and wandering naked through the neighborhood. Sometimes the neighborhood bullies would tease and chase him until he would either find a safe place to hide or make it to Tilly's house. Shug or Pookie had often found June Bug, frightened and trembling behind a dumpster. Several other times, Tilly had escorted him home.

Having suffered from diarrhea all morning, Pookie was not prepared to face Johnny. Reluctantly, ignoring Shug's words, she remained hidden in the rancid-smelling bathroom.

Shug unplugged the iron and went outdoors where she found June Bug, sitting nude in his wagon. He had defecated and smeared it all over his body with his discarded clothes. June Bug's attempt at independence had failed once again.

Johnny followed Shug to the front porch. He stood at the door before sitting down on the stoop. He then watched as she connected the water hose to the outside faucet and turned it on. Shug took June Bug by his hand and led him to the end of the hose, where she began to shower him.

As Pookie reflected on Shug and Johnny's earlier conversation, she thought, "I would love to get a job so I can save money and leave Alabaster, but I'd never return to high school."

High school was the last place Pookie wanted to return. Her classmates had often teased her about her outdated clothes and poverty-stricken neighborhood. Pookie's neighbors were mostly jobless men and women who spent most of their days leaning against graffiti-decorated walls, drinking cheap wine, and gossiping. Unwed teenage mothers, carrying their crying and hungry babies on their hips, walked around in search of some type of child support from the deadbeat fathers. Even with Mrs. Roberson's hand-me-down clothes and an occasional loan from Reverend Horace Hurley, Shug barely earned enough to pay rent or buy food. Pookie knew it would take a lot of luck for her to escape being added to the list of neighborhood failures.

Pookie, believing that she had heard Johnny drive away, went into the kitchen to get the wet clothes out of the washer. She stepped into a puddle of soapy water, leaking from the bottom of their old washing machine.

Pookie took the wet and tangled clothes out of the washer and put them in the clothesbasket. She then took them outdoors through the kitchen door. To her surprise, Johnny was waiting to help her hang clothes on the line. She could barely contain her emotions. The man she fantasized about every night was standing right in front of her.

Pookie's dreams were many, but two constantly remained in her thoughts. Firstly, she aspired to be a famous jazz or blues singer and secondly, she wanted to be Johnny's girlfriend.

The very handsome Johnny, with his infectious smile and gregarious personality, could charm any girl he wanted. This even included her arch nemesis—Reverend Hurley's beautiful daughter, Alspice. That somber realization caused the skinny Pookie to wonder what Johnny could possibly see in her.

Shug finally had June Bug washed off. She was trying to get him to go back into the house so she could dress him in some clean clothes. However, the twenty-five year old man with the mind of a two-year-old child refused and began to throw a temper tantrum.

June Bug's loud cries got the attention of Pookie and Johnny, causing their eyes to momentarily fixate on his hairy chest and erect penis. Pookie simultaneously glanced at Johnny's chest and crotch, wondering if similar things were hiding underneath his baggy shirt and tight jeans. Finally forcing the nude and wet June Bug to cooperate, Shug escorted him into the house.

"So… you want to sing gospel, professionally?" Johnny asked, breaking the silence.

"Who told you that?"

"Your mother told me. I've heard you sing, too."

"Where?"

"At your church."

"I've never seen you at Mount Holy."

"I only live two houses down the street from Mount Holy. When my bedroom window is open, I can hear you singing on plenty of those hot Sunday mornings."

"I sing that loud?"

"With your deep, sultry voice… you'd have no trouble becoming a successful blues artist. If I didn't know you, I wouldn't believe such a beautiful voice came from such a skinny, boyish-looking girl."

"Why do you think I look like a boy?" Pookie asked, her face turning bright red.

"Because you're tall and skinny."

"And…."

"Well… your head is too little for your thick, curly hair. And besides… you don't have any bosom."

"Then don't waste your time with an ugly girl like me!"

"Now hear me out," Johnny said, attempting to calm down the insulted Pookie. "With your talent and the right kind of clothes and make-up, you could be famous. All it will take is some money so you can catch that train to Chicago with me!"

"I don't have any money and you don't either."

"Take that job at Bill's Hardware and save your money like I'm doing," Johnny insisted.

"Working there will allow you to see me. That is… if I'm not playing my guitar or performing at Bettie's Blues Barn."

"Becoming a professional blues singer is a dream of mine, but Shug would be so disappointed in me."

"It's your future, Pookie. You should be the one to decide what you want to do."

"But…."

"I'm coming to Mount Holy on one of these Sunday mornings to hear you sing in person. If you're as good as I think you are, we'll catch that train to Chicago together!"

"Why Chicago?"

"As a matter of fact, we can go to Chicago, Detroit, or New York. All of the big time music producers and record companies are located in one of those three cities. That's why!"

"Big time producers and record companies like who?"

"Well in Chicago… Vee-Jay Records produced 'For Your Precious Love' for Jerry Butler and The Impressions and 'The Shoop Shoop Song' for Betty

Everett. They also signed and recorded The Beatles. Chicago has Chess Records that produced 'Rescue Me' for Fontella Bass and "At Last' for Etta James. There's even OKeh Records, which produces Curtis Mayfield."

"And Detroit?"

"Detroit has one of the biggest music producers ever. Berry Gordy works with Smokey Robinson and The Miracles, the Supremes, Marvin Gaye, the Temptations, the Four Tops, Gladys Knight and the Pips, and the Commodores. Heck girl! There's too many to name."

"Who's in New York?"

"Well… I don't know much about New York. But, I do know that ABC-Paramount is based there and they record a lot of Chicago acts like The Impressions, who are led by Curtis Mayfield, as well as The Marvelows. Brunswick is another New York-based label that produces a lot of Chicago-style soul like Jackie Wilson's 'Your Love Keeps Lifting Me Higher' and The Chi-Lites 'Oh Girl'."

"It seems like you've done your homework. But, I'm just not sure."

"Trust me, Pookie. The record companies I named

can make us rich and famous overnight just like they've already done for countless other artists. I even know some personally."

"If you know so many people who can make you rich and famous, why aren't you there with them instead of here in Alabaster?"

"I'm just waiting for the right time," Johnny retorted.

"Is there ever a right time?"

"Then, what are you waiting for?" Johnny asked, turning the question back on Pookie. "Don't you want to ride that train to fame with me?"

"I do want a chance," Pookie answered, contemplating if she really had the talent to transition from a gospel singer at her small church into a renowned recording artist.

"Then come with me," Johnny said, listening to the whistles of a distant train. "Let's leave this godforsaken town and make a future together."

The determination in his spellbinding ebony eyes mesmerized Pookie. She looked directly at him and said, "I promise to think about it some more later."

"Well… Pookie McAdoo… my mind is made up! I'll be on that train and if you're not with me, I'll just have to hum 'I'm Gonna Miss You' by The Artistics as I think about you.

"Pookie," Shug called loudly, interrupting their conversation. "Have you finished hanging the clothes out to dry?"

"Yes, ma'am," Pookie answered, coming back to reality after realizing that Shug could hear her and Johnny's conversation.

"I heard you trying to sweet talk my daughter," Shug said, laughing as she walked over and leaned against her dilapidated Chevrolet.

Shug had changed her clothes. She was no longer wearing her old frumpy housedress. She was now wearing a pair of jeans, one of Mr. Roberson's white shirts, and a pair of tennis shoes. Her thick black hair was neatly combed. The evening shade cast a shadow against Shug's beautiful brown face, making her appear younger than her teenaged daughter.

"I don't want to be rude, Johnny, but my daughter is a God-fearing girl. I hope she has a future singing religious songs. She doesn't need to be running anywhere with a twenty something year old man like yourself. You're a stock boy, in a hardware store, and you play a guitar at Bettie's Blues Barn. You don't have anything to offer my daughter!"

"One of these days, I'm going to be famous," Johnny replied, stunned by Shug's criticisms.

"I know, Johnny," Shug teased while getting into her car and rolling down the windows. "I've heard it all before about how small-town southern folks always want to go to one of those big cities in hope of making it big. But, they forget that no matter where they go… they will always have to take themselves with them. And that lesson goes for you too—'Mister I'm going to be famous.'" She then looked at Pookie and said, "Listen out for June Bug. He's asleep in his bed. I'm going to the store to buy some chicken to fry for church tomorrow. Have the kitchen cleaned by the time I get back!"

"Yes, ma'am," Pookie responded.

"I guess I need to be going," Johnny said, leaving Pookie standing by the clothesline.

"You better!" Shug said. "I'm not leaving you here."

"Don't forget to buy some sugar," Pookie said, leaving the clothesbasket on the ground and sitting on the stoop. "I want to sweeten my blackberries."

"Where did you find blackberries?" Shug asked, perplexed.

"Down by the old railroad tracks."

"That's where the tramps camp!" Shug shouted. "Don't go down there, again! Do you hear me?"

"Yes, ma'am," Pookie responded, unhappy to be treated like a child in front of Johnny.

Pookie had, however, already decided against returning to the railroad tracks. Two homeless homosexual tramps that camped together near there did not like her picking their blackberries. To teach her a lesson, they peed on the berry bush as she watched in horror.

Johnny said goodbye and then drove away. Shug quickly followed, leaving behind a cloud of gas fumes.

The fumes reminded Pookie of one of her recurring dreams. In her nightmare, her and Shug would be chatting as they rode in the Chevrolet. Suddenly, the car would stall in the middle of the highway. As Shug turned the key, in an attempt to restart the engine, the car ignited into flames. Although she and Shug would always escape the inferno, June Bug would be left screaming and burning in the back seat. Pookie would always awaken after her and Shug were safely by the side of the road, laughing as June Bug burned to death. Drenched in sweat and visibly shaken, Pookie could never fathom why the dream portrayed her and Shug as being happy to have the retarded June Bug out of their lives.

To block out the horrible thoughts, Pookie decided to revisit her and Johnny's conversation about becoming rich and famous.

She twirled around and said, "I want to hear my voice on all the rhythm-and-blues radio stations."

After much reflection, Pookie decided to take the evening job at Bill's Hardware in order to save money so she could move to Chicago, Detroit, or New York with Johnny. She had no doubt that they would become stars and have futures as beautiful as the setting sun.

However, the hunger pangs that twisted inside her guts refocused her attention back to her current situation. She was a high-school dropout, living in a poor neighborhood full of druggies, drunks, and losers.

Would riding that train with Johnny make a difference? Or was she just like the small-town country folks that Shug had described? Was it possible that she, too, was running away from herself while not realizing that no matter where she went, she would have to take herself?

*   *   *   *   *

Pookie heard her next-door neighbor, Mr. Jesse Chappelle, opening his front door. Through the cracks of his tall wooden fence, she watched as he walked to his mailbox. Being a creature of habit, he would do this at the same time everyday.

Pookie wanted to greet him, but Mr. Jesse had become a hermitic recluse. He was once an outgoing man that baked some of the best chocolate brownies, which he would share with her, June Bug, and the two sissy tramps. But that all changed once his wife, Mrs. Ruby, left him. Soon afterwards, he stopped visiting and speaking to everyone in the neighborhood.

It was a surprise that the couple had remained together as long as they did. They did not have much, if anything, in common.

Mr. Jesse was a short man with thick-rimmed glasses. Seven days a week, he would wear the same drab outfit—a grey suit, white shirt, and brown shoes. He was nothing like his wife.

Mrs. Ruby was one of the most beautiful women in Alabaster. She was tall and slender. Her long black hair hung far below her small waist. Her olive skin was flawless and her makeup was always carefully done. She wore only ruby-red lipstick on her full lips. Her clothes clung seductively to her body.

Regardless of their differences, it was obvious that Mr. Jesse truly loved and adored Mrs. Ruby.

They had befriended Shug as soon as she had moved into the house next door. Ruby's best friend, Tilly, also greeted Shug with open arms. Mrs. Ruby and Tilly had even encouraged Shug to join their church, Mount Holy. Soon after joining, Shug was baptized by the pastor, Reverend Horace Hurley. Against Pookie's will, he also baptized her and June Bug.

As a faithful and long-term member of Mount Holy, Mrs. Ruby volunteered to be secretary for the church. Her pudgy and unassuming husband, Mr. Jesse, would go home alone as she began to work longer and longer hours during the weekdays and weekends with Reverend Hurley.

The beginning of the end of their marriage came when Mrs. Ruby announced that she was pregnant. Mr. Jesse was so ecstatic that he baked and delivered brownies to Pookie and June Bug when he came to share the good news with Shug. He bragged to Shug that if the baby were a boy, he would name him Jesse Chappelle, Jr. and if a girl, he would name her Amy Lee after his dearly departed mother.

However, instead of exhibiting Mr. Jesse's excitement, Mrs. Ruby had grown distant from her husband. She eventually distanced herself from even Tilly and Shug.

Mrs. Ruby and Mr. Jesse began to get into loud arguments. Mr. Jesse would be begging her to stay home with him and to take care of their unborn child in lieu of volunteering at Mount Holy for Reverend Hurley.

One day, Mrs. Ruby had had enough of Mr. Jesse's pleading. Pookie, who would often sit by the kitchen window and listen, could hear their every word.

"It's not your baby!" Mrs. Ruby said angrily.

"Just because you're upset with me, there's no reason to be cruel!"

"What did Dr. Harry tell us?"

"Dr. Harry told us that our baby would be born in six months."

"Fool, can't you count?" Mrs. Ruby screamed.

"When was the last time you had your little prick in me?"

The silence coming from the Chappelle's house seemed to last for an eternity. Desperately wanting to hear Mr. Jesse's response, Pookie stood closer to the window and listened carefully.

"If it's not my baby, then whose is it?" Mr. Jesse asked, disappointed and shocked.

"Why?"

"I have the right to know! That's why!"

"I don't care," Mrs. Ruby shouted, sounding exhausted and irate. "I'm not going to tell you!"

"Yes… you… are!" Mr. Jesse said with his voice stuttering.

"Take your stubby little hands off me!" Mrs. Ruby said, screaming and crying to the top of her voice. "You're hurting me!"

"Tell me!" Mr. Jesse pleaded. "Tell me who fathered our child!"

"Let me go!" Mrs. Ruby begged. "You're hurting me!"

"Tell me who fathered our child!"

Pookie then heard inaudible sounds followed by deafening silence. No matter how attentively she listened, she could not make out what answer Mrs. Ruby gave to Mr. Jesse's question regarding the paternity of their child.

On the next day after their argument, Mr. Jesse came over to tell Shug that a pregnant Mrs. Ruby had abandoned him and was not coming back. He then gave Shug a platter of chocolate brownies to give to Pookie and June Bug. It would be the last time he would bake them or come over to visit.

It was rumored amongst the neighbors that Mr. Jesse had killed Mrs. Ruby in a fit of jealous rage and buried her under their house upon learning of her infidelity. It was also rumored that Reverend Hurley was actually the one who fathered her unborn child.

Although a self-professed God-fearing man, that would not be the last child that Reverend Hurley was rumored to have sired while married to his wife, Mrs. Pearl.

After Mrs. Ruby supposedly left, Tilly became Reverend Hurley's personal secretary. Shug began to see less and less of her friend. Once when she and Tilly were sitting on the stoop, Tilly confided in Shug that she was in love with, and four months pregnant by, a married man. Shug asked Tilly the man's name, but she had promised to keep his name a secret until he fulfilled his promise to divorce his wife and marry her.

When Tilly's pregnancy became neighborhood gossip, the Deacon Board of Mount Holy held an emergency meeting. The decision was made to ask Tilly to leave the church and join another one where she was unknown. They believed that she was a bad influence on the younger church members. Tilly was advised to lie to her new church by claiming that her husband had died of cancer or was killed in a car accident.

Tilly was heartbroken, especially after Reverend Hurley refused to override their decision. He even refused to take her calls or to pray for her salvation. Not only was Tilly kicked out of Mount Holy, but also the man she loved deserted her.

Tilly went into seclusion until her daughter, Tammy Sue, was born due to the embarrassment of having a bastard child. Having also been ostracized from the church she had attended since she was a child, Tilly had started to drink excessively. She was a caricature of her former self. Tilly, a woman that once had an immaculate appearance and was a pillar of the community, now walked the streets of Alabaster like a homeless hobo.

As Pookie watched Mr. Jesse disappear back into his house with his mail, she saw Shug walking towards their house. She was carrying two large bags of groceries.

Pookie went to open the door and help her with the bags.

"Where's the car?" Pookie asked, surprised that Shug was returning home on foot.

"It stopped running on me, again," Shug answered. "Is June Bug still asleep?"

"Yes, ma'am."

"That's good! I have enough going on already!"

"Since the car isn't running, will we have to ride to church tomorrow with the Hurley family?"

"Yes, we will!" Shug snapped. "They're good God-fearing folks."

"Why do we have to fear God?" Pookie asked, looking inside one of the grocery bags.

"Ask the Reverend, tomorrow! If you're looking for

sugar, I didn't buy any."

"Why?"

"I didn't have enough money."

"Can I borrow some from Miss Tilly?"

"No!"

"Why not?"

"Tilly is a drunk! Stay away from her before you become one, too."

"She wasn't a drunk until those heathens and Reverend Hurley backstabbed her!"

"I told Mr. Bill that you'd take that job at his store," Shug said, changing the subject. "You can help me pay bills and buy food with the money you earn."

Pookie did not want to use her hard-earned money to help pay bills or buy extra food. She wanted to work and save her money so she could buy a train ticket and leave with Johnny. But for now, she decided to keep her future plans a secret.

She and Shug set the grocery bags on the dirty floor because Pookie had forgotten to clean the kitchen. Food-stained breakfast dishes were still on the counter and table. A pot, used to cook oatmeal, and a greasy cast-iron skillet, used to fry eggs and ham, were in the sink. Shug must have been extremely exhausted because she did not fuss about the mess. Instead, she took a stick of coconut candy out of her back pocket and handed it to Pookie, who ate it in three big bites before discarding the wrapper onto the floor.

Pookie then opened the kitchen door and tossed her bowl of withered blackberries into the yard.

She suddenly heard a train in the distance, making a choo-choo sound as it moved down the tracks.

"Will I ever ride that train?" Pookie thought aloud.

"What did you say?" Shug asked, taking raw chickens out of the bags and putting them into the refrigerator. "Were you talking to me?"

"No, ma'am. I was just thinking out loud."

"Why did you throw away your berries? Didn't you want them?"

"Not really," Pookie answered, setting the blackberry juice-stained bowl on top of the stove. "Those two sissy tramps urinated on the bushes."

"At least they have each other," Shug said, picking up the discarded candy wrapper off the floor and putting it into the garbage can. "They aren't dying of loneliness like our poor neighbor, Mr. Jesse."

"Do you think he still takes brownies to them?"

"I doubt it. Besides checking his mail, he's rarely seen outside of his house."

"I just saw him outside before you walked up."

"I sure do miss the friendship me, Jesse, and Ruby once had. Heck… if Tilly stopped drinking… maybe we could go back to how we used to be."

"Have you tried to talk to Mr. Jesse?"

"Many times," Shug answered, as she closed the refrigerator door.

"Have you tried to get Tilly to stop drinking?"

"Are you hungry?" Shug asked, ignoring Pookie's inquiry.

"No, ma'am. That candy killed my appetite."

"Well… don't make a habit out of missing meals."

"If you don't mind… I'm going to bed."

"Wait for me! I might as well get some rest while June Bug is still asleep. We got a long day ahead of us."

"Reverend Hurley can be long-winded," Pookie responded as she waited for Shug. "Why should I go to church, if I don't believe in God?"

"You have to believe if you want to enter into God's kingdom," Shug replied, putting a few cans of vegetables into the kitchen cabinet. "Don't you want to go to heaven when you die?"

"I don't know. I've never been to heaven before."

"Heaven is a good place to go."

"Have you been to heaven?"

"Don't be silly," Shug answered, almost laughing. "I've never been dead."

"Then, how would you know it's a good place to go?"

"The Bible tells us so!"

"Why should I believe what the Bible says?"

"The Bible is the truth!"

"You told me not to believe everything that I read."

"Pookie McAdoo… that's blasphemy! If you don't change your thoughts, you're going to burn in hell!"

"Isn't being fatherless, poor, living in government housing, and having a retarded brother already like living in hell?"

"June Bug's problems are the result of my sins," Shug said, as if she may have found some truth within Pookie's words.

"If they're your sins, why did God have to punish June Bug?"

Pookie's question went unanswered. From the expression on Shug's face, she decided not to press her luck.

On their way to their bedroom, Shug and Pookie stopped to check on June Bug. Shug went inside his room as Pookie waited patiently by the door. Shug would always keep June Bug's door ajar so that she could hear him in the event he cried out for her during the night.

As always, June Bug had kicked his blanket off the

bed. Pookie watched as Shug took the blanket off the floor and gently placed it around his frail body and large head.

Shug then left June Bug's room and she and Pookie continued to the bedroom they shared.

Shug changed into her cotton nightgown, turned off the light, and got into bed. Pookie was left to undress using only the illumination of the streetlights that shone through their dusty bedroom window.

Pookie then laid down next to Shug with their backs touching. Soon, they would have to awaken to another uncertain day.

"Good night, Mama."

"Good night, Pookie."

After several minutes of silence, Pookie heard Shug whispering her prayers.

She prayed, "God forgive me for my sins, prove your existence to my nonbelieving daughter, Pookie, and keep my helpless son, June Bug, safe."

Soon afterwards, she dosed off to sleep.

Except for Shug's soft snoring and June Bug restlessly turning in his bed, all was quiet inside their small, hot house.

The same could not, however, be said about the noises coming from their impoverished slum of a neighborhood. Mouths full of curse words, drunkards stumbling home, and petty arguments echoed throughout the night as they slept.

Pookie tuned out the loud noises, allowing her tense body to relax. She was momentarily startled by the familiarity of a sound approaching from the far distance. It was the humming of another northern-bound train, whistling her name as it passed in the night.

CHAPTER 4

June Bug, wearing his only suit, was almost ready for church. He stared with curiosity into the mirror, looking at his image as Pookie combed his thinning hair. His top teeth were yellowish and protruded over his bottom lip. They had several cavities, causing his breath to reek. Shug, low on money, had decided to ask Reverend Hurley for a loan so she could have all of his teeth extracted.

When Pookie finished combing his hair, she insisted that he stay seated in his room while she went and got dressed. Shug did not want June Bug to see her or Pookie naked. Even though he had the mind of a child, his body was fully mature.

As Pookie was putting on her stockings, she caught June Bug peeping into her room. She called out to Shug, who was frying chicken and biscuits in the kitchen. Shug hurried into Pookie's room. She pointed the large fork that she had been using to fry chicken at June Bug and told him to stop spying on his sister.

After scolding June Bug, Shug took him into the kitchen and sat him at the table. She gave him a fried buttered biscuit. As always, butter dripped onto his blue suit. Shug took her dishrag and attempted to wipe the greasy stain away.

Pookie—dressed in a navy blue skirt, white blouse, and white patent-leather pumps—then came into the kitchen to help Shug cook. But, by that time, Shug had already finished and had put the greasy food into two paper bags.

With the food and everyone ready, they sat at the kitchen table and waited for Reverend and Mrs. Hurley to come and drive them to church.

Reverend Hurley drove his station wagon into their driveway and honked the horn. Although Shug and Pookie hurried out of their seats, June Bug remained seated. Shug took the bags of food off the table, being careful not to get grease on her white suit. She told Pookie to bring her brother outside.

Pookie took June Bug by his hand to lead him to the car, but he would not budge. Even when she continued to pull, he still did not budge. It was as if he had glued himself to the cushion of the chair.

June Bug could be very stubborn and strong when he did not want to cooperate. Neither Shug nor Pookie could make him do anything when his mind was made up.

Shug, noticing that June Bug was still not cooperating, instead handed the bags to Pookie. She told her to take the food out to the car and to ask Reverend Hurley to come inside to help her with June Bug.

Before Pookie left, Shug reminded her to say good morning to the Hurley's and not get grease on her clothes. Pookie left Shug in the kitchen with June Bug while she went outside, carrying the chicken fat saturated bags to greet the Hurley's.

Reverend Hurley and Mrs. Pearl had all the windows rolled down in their station wagon as they impatiently waited in the August heat. Pookie wanted to turn around and run back into the house, but thoughts of Shug's wrath would not permit her.

Reverend Hurley looked like a teddy bear stuffed into a too small black suit. He unloosened his red tie and unbuttoned the top button on his white shirt. Because it was the third Sunday, he did not want to be late for church. Mount Holy would be filled to its capacity with adults and children. On this particular day, parishioners would be prepared to tithe a lot of their hard-earned money. In addition, tables in the basement of the church would be covered with platters of soul food in celebration.

Mrs. Pearl's overpowering perfume began to attract buzzing bumblebees. They flew in and out of the car windows as they whirled around her large flowered straw hat, trying to suck nectar from the artificial flowers that decorated it. She frantically waved her arms and hands to fan the bees away as Reverend Hurley helped.

As they chatted, neither of them noticed that Pookie was standing within earshot.

"The McAdoo's always keep us waiting," Reverend Hurley said loudly. "If they don't hurry up, our food is going to spoil and won't be fit to eat. If I weren't a Christian, I'd let them walk! They're probably late because of that idiot, June Bug!"

"Calm down, Horace. Hopefully, Shug's car will be fixed soon."

"Do you know why her son's retarded?"

"No… I don't," Mrs. Pearl said, continuing to swat at the bees.

"Shug told me in secret that June Bug was her…."

"If Shug confided in you," Mrs. Pearl interrupted, "she certainly didn't mean for you to tell me!"

"What a pious woman you have become. You've always been nosy about everyone else's business. But now, all of a sudden, you're acting modest."

"Don't let your big mouth get you into trouble, Horace. Remember Mount Holy is the church that my father, the Honorable Reverend Featherstone, willed to me. I can kick you out anytime I want."

"Stop saying my name after every sentence," Reverend Hurley retorted, smashing a bee with a Mount Holy church fan. "What do you mean about kicking me out of my church?"

"Parishioners are beginning to talk! If they decide to change preachers, all they have to do is convince the board members, which consists of my sisters, Portia and Priscilla, and my brother, Tyrone, and you will be out! The only reason they've kept you this long is because of their love for me and their dedication to our father. If it wasn't for me, your fat ass would be standing behind a plow again!"

"My ouster would mean you would have to stop buying all of your expensive clothes and big hats and there would be no money for Alspice's college education."

"Oh really?"

"Yeah, really! So, shut your mouth or I'll ...."

"Or you'll what, Horace? Put me out of my house? The house where my brother, sisters, and I were born and raised? The house our father left us?"

"As your husband, I became the head of the household after your father died," Reverend Hurley said, slightly raising his voice. "And I've been a damn good husband, going far past what most men would tolerate, especially from an ungrateful wife. I've taken care of you, your spinster twin sisters, and your sissified brother."

"You haven't done a thing, but been a big bully!"

"Look, Pearl! What's wrong with you on this holy Sunday of the month? You've been bitching at me all morning!"

"You don't even know what day it is?"

"Ummm... it's the third Sunday in August. That's what day it is."

"It's our dearly departed son's twentieth birthday, Horace," Mrs. Pearl responded through tears. "Why did he take his own life? Why did he take his grandfather's shotgun and blow his brains out?" Was it because Katherine's baby wasn't his?"

"I should've shaved this morning," Reverend Hurley said, looking in his rear view mirror and quickly changing the subject after noticing that Pookie was listening.

"Were you listening to me and my wife's conversation?"

"No, sir!"

"Where's your mama and brother? It's hot out here!"

"They're in the house. June Bug won't come out."

"That's no reason for you to be standing at the rear of my car, eavesdropping! Go in your house and help your mama!"

"She sent me to ask you to come and help her."

Without saying another word, Reverend Hurley forced his derrière out from under his steering wheel. He took off his hat and set it on his black robe, which was lying across his seat and hurried into the house.

Mrs. Pearl told Pookie to get into the car and put Shug's food on the back seat next to her potato salad and coconut cake. The word food reminded Pookie of what Shug had said, but it was too late. The bags of chicken and biscuits had rubbed against her white blouse, leaving a large stain.

Mrs. Pearl and Pookie waited only a few moments before Reverend Hurley, Shug, and June Bug emerged from the house. As Shug followed, Reverend Hurley forcefully led June Bug down the stoop and to the station wagon. He opened the car door and pushed the uncooperative June Bug inside.

Reluctantly, June Bug sat between Pookie and Shug. He continued to scream as he kicked the back of the seat. He only stopped when Pookie held his hand. Eventually, June Bug quieted down.

At last, five sweaty people were on their way in a station wagon that smelled of flatulence.

When they arrived at Mount Holy, the choir was singing their last song. It was almost time for Reverend Hurley to give his sermon. He parked near the entrance to the pastoral study and quickly got out. He reached for his robe and hat, but they were not where he had placed them. Everyone, except June Bug, began to search for his belongings until Shug spotted them on the floorboard underneath June Bug's large feet.

Shug retrieved the wrinkled robe and squashed hat and gave them to the irate minister. He slammed the door before leaning against his dusty car to put on his robe. Carrying his hat under his sweaty left armpit, he left them sitting in the hot car.

Shug and Mrs. Pearl took their food into the dining area through the basement door. Pookie led June Bug up the steps, through the front door, and into the crowded church. They had to walk all the way to the front pews before finding enough space for them and Shug to sit.

Shug and Pearl eventually came upstairs and joined the congregation. Shug sat next to Pookie and June Bug while Mrs. Pearl sat across the aisle with her daughter, Alspice.

"Look behind you," Shug said, whispering into Pookie's ear. "Look who's sitting in the fourth pew."

"Why?"

"For just once in your life, can you do something that I ask you without asking me why?"

Pookie turned around to look before nervously asking, "Why is Johnny here?"

"It's eating day. This is the only time some people come to church."

"Like Alspice?"

"Pearl told me that Alspice is very sickly so she can't attend church every Sunday."

"She doesn't look sickly to me. She just looks overfed. Maybe she doesn't want to hear her daddy preach what he doesn't practice."

"Why do you talk so negatively about a man called by God to preach?"

"I forgot, Reverend Hurley was plowing in the cotton field early one morning when he…."

"Stop talking that way! I'm going to get Reverend Hurley to minister to you."

"Like he ministered to Mrs. Ruby and Tilly when they got pregnant with his baby?"

"That's not true; those are just rumors!"

"Well… I know one thing that's true."

"And what's that, Miss Pookie McAdoo?"

"You shouldn't let Reverend Hurley spank June Bug."

"Reverend Hurley is only following the Bible, which clearly states that if you spare the rod, you spoil the child. This even applies to a retarded child like your brother, June Bug."

"June Bug is not a child!" Pookie said angrily, forgetting that Johnny was sitting behind her. "He's a man!"

"Shhh!" Shug said, quieting down the irritated Pookie. "Sisters Priscilla and Portia and Brother Tyrone Featherstone are about to start the prayer service."

It was the first time that Pookie hoped that the long-winded prayer warriors, as they called themselves, would take longer than usual. She wanted Johnny to get so bored and hot that he would leave before she was called to sing her solo. But, today, Reverend Hurley's thoughts were on counting his earnings from the tithes of his hard-working church members and tantalizing the food downstairs. Looking flustered, he walked up to the podium and interrupted Brother Tyrone in the middle of his inspirational prayer.

"Thanks Brother Tyrone for those inspirational words. You may now be seated."

"I haven't finished!"

"It's too hot in here for these young babies," Reverend Hurley insisted as Brother Tyrone reluctantly took his seat. "We're going to move things along more quickly this Sunday." Leaning his weight against the podium, he then said, "Now we'll have a solo by Miss Pookie McAdoo."

"Excuse me Reverend, but neither my sister, brother, or I have had a chance to get up and speak," Sister Priscilla said in defiance.

"Priscilla," Reverend Hurley said while beckoning Pookie to come forward, "before this day is over, I assure you that you will have your say."

"Yes, sir," Sister Priscilla responded, obviously competing with Pookie for visibility.

"Miss McAdoo," Reverend Hurley said, "let our congregation hear your lovely voice."

Although nervous, Pookie stood up from her seat. Her half size too small shoes seemed even smaller. Shug gave her a nudge on her butt to help her begin what, as she walked, seemed like a very long journey to the podium.

Pookie was hoping that when she turned to face her audience that Johnny would be gone. But when she glanced out into the crowded church, he was the first person she noticed. She had sung many solos, but today was different. The man she loved was watching.

With Raymond on the drums and Sister Gussie Johnson on the piano, Pookie closed her eyes and began to sing. Her voice trembled for the first few moments before it got stronger and stronger. The parishioners began to shout, "Praise be to our Lord and Savior, Jesus Christ." Some members even caught the Holy Ghost and began to dance in the aisles while others rolled around the floor, panting and fainting.

When Pookie opened her eyes, she looked directly at Johnny. He was using his blue cap to wipe sweat from his forehead. The gray wool suit he was wearing was too hot for the sultry August day.

Pookie's fixated stare got the attention of Mrs. Pearl, who was curious to see who had Pookie's undivided attention. Looking directly back at Johnny caused the brim of her large hat to hit Mrs. Lula Goodson's granddaughter, Pauline, in the eye. When Little Pauline began to cry, June Bug followed suit. As Pookie's toes also began to cry, her singing voice got louder and louder. Most of the congregation was shouting while others followed Mrs. Pearl eyes toward Johnny. This forced him to jump up in discomfort and flee outside.

While everyone was in frenzy, Pookie quickly ended her solo before slipping out of the side door to search for him.

Johnny pressed his back against the church's brick wall. He pulled his blue cap securely over his head and kicked the ground with the heel of his new black shoes. He took a handkerchief from his coat pocket and wiped sweat from his handsome face.

Pookie slowly walked over to Johnny, giving herself enough time to think of what to say. When he saw her approaching him, he tried to put his handkerchief back in his pocket, but it fell on the ground. Pookie picked up his dirty handkerchief with two fingers and handed it back to him. Johnny grabbed the stained cloth from her and returned it to his pocket.

"I'm surprised to see you here," Pookie said. "I didn't see your red truck."

"I left it parked in my yard. I told you that I live two houses down from Mount Holy. I decided to just get dressed and walk up here so I could listen to you sing."

"Really?"

"You sounded really good," Johnny said, looking down at the ground. "Would you be interested in singing at Bettie's Blues Barn?"

"Didn't my mama tell you about filling my head up with foolishness? If you're going to tease me, I'm going back in the church."

"I'm not teasing you. I'm serious. I want you to catch that train to stardom with me."

"My mama would kill me!"

"Aren't you old enough to make some decisions on your own? How old are you anyway?"

Before Pookie could answer his question, she heard June Bug screaming. He was hungry, tired, and asking to go home.

Pookie had constantly asked Shug if she could stay home on Sundays with June Bug in lieu of going to church. But, she would not allow her. Shug believed that if June Bug did not attend, he would not go to heaven when he died.

"I better go back inside," Pookie reluctantly said. "June Bug is acting up."

"Go and get him and bring him out here with us. I'll help you with him."

"If you stay and eat...."

"They don't want me eating their food."

"Why?"

"I'm not a member of Mount Holy."

"You're welcome to eat the food we brought."

"What did you bring?"

"We have fried chicken and fried biscuits."

"I love fried chicken, but I've never heard of fried biscuits."

"Well... this is your chance to try some."

"I just might do that."

"Wait right here and I'll go and get June Bug."

Before Pookie could go to get June Bug, Reverend Hurley appeared at the door with him. The angry preacher called out to Pookie for her to keep her brother outside and to make him be quiet. Reverend Hurley then returned to the church.

Pookie and Johnny led June Bug across the churchyard to a bench under a large sycamore tree. When Pookie saw the sad look on her brother's face, she began to hate Reverend Hurley and Mount Holy.

Pookie told June Bug to sit on the bench, but he would not. With Johnny's help, she tried to force him. However, they could not force the rigid June Bug to sit or to stop crying until he reached and pulled the cap off of Johnny's head. Pookie tried to get the cap away from him, but he held on tighter. Johnny told Pookie to let June Bug keep it for a while. When Pookie did, June Bug finally sat on the bench, stopped crying, and put Johnny's cap on his gigantic head.

With June Bug in the middle, Pookie and Johnny also sat on the bench. They took a deep sigh of relief before almost falling asleep from the boredom of listening to the preaching, singing, testifying, and shouting that emanated from inside the church.

Their tranquility, however, did not last long. When June Bug saw Reverend and Mrs. Hurley, he began to hit Pookie in the face with Johnny's cap. They were coming from the church's basement carrying their plates, which were running over with food. Mrs. Pearl held Reverend Hurley's and her plate as he placed two folding chairs under the weeping willow tree. They then sat and began to eat.

Mrs. Pearl's twin sisters, Priscilla and Portia, and her brother, Tyrone, detested their brother-in-law, Reverend Horace Hurley. They were beginning to think that he possessed too much power over the church that their father, Reverend Featherstone, founded and pastored. They also felt he was too overpowering with their sister, Mrs. Pearl. They wanted Reverend Hurley expelled from Mount Holy and hopefully from their sister's life. If their names were on the deed to the church, Reverend Hurley, with or without Mrs. Pearl's consent, would have been out of the podium a long time ago.

Mrs. Pearl was forced into marrying Reverend Hurley. When she met him, he was a raggedy, dirty-looking stranger who had wandered into the small farming town of Alabaster. After being homeless on the streets for four years, he was looking for a place to live and work. He asked someone in town where he could seek help and was advised to ask Reverend Featherstone.

Reverend Hurley told Reverend Featherstone that at the age of six, he discovered his mother dead on her bedroom floor. Motherless and with no other relatives willing to take him in, he had lived in seven different foster homes until he was eighteen.

Being a good Christian, Reverend Featherstone took the twenty-two year old stranger into his home.

However, the first day he and the then sixteen-year-old Mrs. Pearl set eyes on each other, Reverend Featherstone believed that he had made a mistake. But Reverend Featherstone, being a widower with three teenage daughters and a baby son to rear while working on his farm and preaching on Sundays, needed someone to help him tend to the fields and the animals. So, he gave Horace a chance. In exchange for food, a place to sleep in the hayloft, and a small salary—he was hired to feed the animals and plow and plant the fields. Instead, Reverend Hurley stayed in the barn, rolling around in the hay, planting his seeds in Mrs. Pearl.

After coming home one evening from ministering to a sick friend, Reverend Featherstone caught his twin girls outside of the house. The innocent thirteen-year-old twins, Priscilla and Portia, were looking through a peephole in the barn. When the girls saw their father, they took off running back toward their small house. Reverend Featherstone told his daughters to stop running and to wait for him. The girls knew to never disobey their father. He asked them why were they peeping inside the barn instead of helping their sister, Pearl, care for their baby brother, Tyrone, and cooking supper. He said that they had better have a good answer or they would get a whipping that they would never forget. His sharp words were all the girls needed to hear because they knew Reverend Featherstone did not believe in sparing the rod.

“Looking at Pearl and Horace,” the girls admitted simultaneously.

“At who and who,” Reverend Featherstone asked, not believing what he had just heard.

“At Pearl and Horace,” the twins repeated.

“Pearl’s not in the house?” Reverend Tyrone asked, his voice rising with anger.

“No, sir,” Priscilla responded.

“Where’s your brother?” Reverend Featherstone inquired.

“In the house, asleep,” Portia answered.

Reverend Featherstone took a long and slow look over the field where Horace should have been plowing, old Joe, the mule. However, all he saw was old Joe standing under the tall walnut tree and a cloudy sky, indicating that a storm was brewing. He told the girls to go inside the house. The girls quickly complied. As fast as they could, they ran toward the house while occasionally looking back at their father.

Reverend Featherstone waited until the twins were safely inside the house before he went to look through the peephole. What he saw nearly gave him a heart attack. Sixteen-year-old Pearl and the much older, Horace, were having sex on top of a bale of hay. For Reverend Featherstone, that was the last straw. With his bare hands, he pulled a rotten plank off the side of the barn, leaving a space, which he used to enter.

When Mrs. Pearl saw her father, she pushed Reverend Hurley off of her. With her panties in her hand, she ran and hid in old Joe's stall. Horace had just enough time to pull up his overalls before Reverend Featherstone grabbed the handle of a broken pitchfork in which he used to viciously beat him. Horace was no match for the enraged, although smaller and older, preacher nicknamed "Midget." Reverend Featherstone beat Horace across his back and head until he knocked him unconscious. The little preacher dragged the bloody faced Horace, by his feet, out of the barn and left him face down in chicken manure while he ran home to get his shotgun.

The twins surmised that Reverend Featherstone was searching for his shotgun when they saw him rummaging through his closet. Fearing what he may do, they clung to his legs and begged him not to kill Horace. Their pleading brought Reverend Featherstone back to his senses, remembering he was a man of God and Thou Shalt Not Kill. If he killed Horace, he would have to answer to God and the law, go to prison, and leave his children fatherless.

Reverend Featherstone then abandoned the search for his shotgun and instructed the twins to cook supper. The girls released their father's legs and went into the kitchen to finish the supper that Pearl had already started. Reverend Featherstone went into his bedroom to lie next to his baby son Tyrone, Jr., leaving Mrs. Pearl hiding in the barn and Reverend Hurley in a puddle of his own blood.

The storm was turning violent as heavy rain tap-danced on the tin roof. Daylight was now turning into darkness and Pearl was still not home. Usually late evenings were the Featherstone's favorite time even on stormy, rainy days. After supper, the twins would normally sit in front of the fireplace, chatting and playing with their homemade dolls. Pearl would wash the dishes while dreaming of leaving the farm one day. And Reverend Featherstone would sit in his rocking chair and hold Tyrone until he went to sleep. But today was not routine; the twins were extremely worried as they prepared supper.

Portia looked out of the kitchen window, toward the barn and the field, in hopes of seeing Pearl or Horace. Everything was pitch black until streaks of lightning momentarily dispelled the darkness. She saw the old mule, Joe, running toward the barn. However, she still did not know the whereabouts of Pearl or Horace.

Reverend Featherstone continued to pace back and forth in his bedroom. The twins knew their father was worried about Pearl, but his pride would never allow him to show it.

The reverend believed only sissies cried or showed weakness. Before her father could come into the kitchen and catch her, Portia hurried away from the window and went back to stir the pinto beans as Priscilla set the table.

"Does the storm look as bad as it sounds?" Priscilla asked, whispering.

"Worse," Portia said, also in a whisper. "Do you think Pearl is all right?"

"I hope so," Priscilla answered.

"Girls… stop whispering and get the food on the table," Reverend Featherstone said, bringing Tyrone, Jr. into the kitchen and sitting him in his highchair.

The Featherstone's were eating their supper when a famished Pearl walked in the kitchen. She reasoned that sooner or later she would have to face her father and take her whipping.

When the twins saw Pearl, looking like a wet hen, they stopped eating. Baby Tyrone continued to kick his feet and draw circles in his food. Reverend Featherstone dropped the cornbread he was taking a bite from into his plate of pinto beans and fried ham. He rubbed his greasy hands across the legs of his best black suit. With his eyes still bloodshot red from anger, he looked at Pearl and over at his well-used black leather strap hanging on the wall. He pushed his chair away from the table and stood, taking his chair with him as he went to get his strap. As he sat back down in his chair, Pearl knew exactly what to do.

Leaving her muddy footprints behind and taking a deep breath, she walked over to her father as she tightened the muscles in her buttocks. She then laid across her father's bony lap.

Reverend Featherstone placed his left hand on the back of Pearl's head, whose long braids touched the floor. Reverend Featherstone looked at Portia and Priscilla, who were nervously anticipating Pearl's whipping. Portia's mouth was filled with ham when Reverend Featherstone called her name. She preferred to take a chance of choking, quickly swallowing the tough meat, rather than giving her father the impression that she was being disrespectful.

"Portia."

"Yes, sir," Portia answered, with a lump of ham barely going down her esophagus and tears in her eyes.

"Priscilla."

"Yes, sir?" Priscilla also answered.

"I want you girls to remember this whipping I'm going to give your defiant sister, Pearl. If you do, you'll be sure to never repeat her sinful mistake!"

"Yes, sir," the twins both said, through crackling voices.

"Maybe even your now tainted sister will give her life to God and choose an ascetic life of prayer, fasting, and tiding," Reverend Featherstone said as he prepared Pearl's butt for the inevitable lashing it would receive.

Reverend Featherstone raised his strap high above his head. But before he could bring it down on Pearl's backside, Horace, looking like a rabid dog, ran into the house. The top of his head to the bottom of his holey shoes was soaked with rainwater. His face looked like he had been shocked by lightning twice and he smelled of chicken manure.

Dumbfounded, Reverend Featherstone pushed Pearl off of his lap, stood up, and lowered the strap to his side. Pearl crawled across the kitchen floor and hid under the table.

Horace ran over to Reverend Featherstone and knelt at his feet. He testified to Reverend Featherstone that he had awakened on the ground, feeling hopeless and near death, until God spared him.

Horace begged Reverend Featherstone to let him marry Pearl and restore her respectability. He promised that from that day forward his sole purpose in life would be to spread the gospel of Jesus Christ.

Feeling this was divine intervention coupled with the realization that Pearl was no longer a virgin, Reverend Featherstone abandoned his plans of an old-fashioned lashing and gave them his blessings for marriage.

Horace, now called Reverend Hurley by all that knew him, and Mrs. Pearl eventually sired two children—a son, Horace Jr., and a daughter, Alspice. After Reverend Featherstone died, he and Mrs. Pearl inherited Mount Holy. With Portia, Priscilla, and Tyrone's names left off of the deed, they were forced to honor their deceased father's wishes.

When Alspice saw Johnny, June Bug, and Pookie

sitting on the bench, she decided to join them. Because there was not enough room for four people on the bench, Johnny gave Alspice his seat.

Alspice was wearing a black skirt that was too short for her large hips. The top two buttons of her red silk blouse were unbuttoned, exposing her voluptuous cleavage. Johnny could not keep his eyes off of her bosom. Even June Bug stared while trying to put his hand down her blouse.

"June Bug… you're a bad boy," Alspice said, grabbing his hand and pushing it away.

"Johnny… let's take June Bug to go and get something to eat," Pookie said, intimidated by Alspice's perky breasts.

"Johnny… Pookie is talking to you," Alspice said, seductively.

"I'm sorry Pookie," Johnny replied, momentarily taking his eyes away from Alspice. "Were you talking to me?"

"I said… let's go and get something to eat before it's all gone."

"You don't have to," Alspice said. "Here comes your mama with two extra plates."

Shug handed Pookie a plate of food and a slice of Mrs. Pearl's coconut cake. She set the other plate, piled high with Mrs. Pearl's potato salad, in June Bug's lap. Because of his decaying teeth, he had to eat soft food and avoid sweets.

June Bug dug his dirty hands into the mound of potato salad. The mayonnaise, eggs, pickles, and potatoes oozed between his fingers. He offered a hand full to Johnny.

"No thank you, June Bug," Johnny said, moving away.

"I'll fix Johnny a plate," Shug said.

"Johnny, did you bring any food today?" Alspice inquired.

"Did you?" Pookie snapped at Alspice.

"My mama did!" Alspice snapped back, pointing her finger at Pookie's plate and at June Bug's potato salad covered hand. "That's my mama's coconut cake on your plate and her potato salad all over your stupid brother's hands!"

"How do you know?" Pookie asked, confrontationally.

"You think I don't recognize my own mama's food," Alspice retorted.

"Please… please," Johnny said, intervening. "I'm not hungry. My uncle, Toby, has dinner waiting for me at home."

"Johnny… you can have some of my chicken and biscuits," Shug said, trying to defuse the tension between Pookie and the Hurley's daughter, the same people who they were depending on for a ride home.

"No, ma'am," Johnny responded, reaching for his cap on June Bug's head. "I must be going."

Johnny took his cap off of June Bug's head and said goodbye. As he readied to walk away, June Bug screamed and threw his potato salad at Alspice. The food splattered all over her. Alspice quickly jumped up and gave Johnny her plate to hold. She tried to clean the food off of her face and blouse, but to no avail. Shug, Pookie, and Johnny watched in astonishment as the oil from the mayonnaise stained her blouse.

Alspice then angrily screamed for her father. Her screams were so loud that a crowd of parishioners began to gather around the commotion. Reverend Hurley and Mrs. Pearl came running toward their daughter's cries for help.

"What happened, Alspice?" Reverend Hurley asked.

"That idiot did it," Alspice cried, pointing her finger so close to June Bug's face that he became cross-eyed. "He ruined my expensive blouse!"

"Shug… I'm about to teach this boy of yours some manners," Reverend Hurley said, handing his empty paper plate to Mrs. Pearl with one hand and removing his black belt with the other.

Upon realizing that Reverend Hurley was preparing to spank June Bug, Pookie threw her plate of food onto the ground, shocking everyone. She made sure to purposely stump on Mrs. Pearl's coconut cake.

When Mrs. Pearl saw what Pookie had done, she almost fainted. June Bug was elated and like a monkey at the zoo, he began to jump up and down. To give the spectators their money's worth, he also began to throw the rest of his potato salad at the crowd of people that had formed around them.

"Reverend Hurley… my brother isn't an idiot or a boy!" Pookie shouted, with her hands on her hips. She stared directly into his eyes, shocking him by the drastic change in her demeanor. "He's a man and he should be respected as such! I want to let you know, right here on this holy ground, that if there is a heaven, June Bug will get there before you do!"

She then took two steps toward the shocked Reverend Hurley before continuing, "If you ever put your hands on my brother again, I will whip your…."

"Pookie," Shug screamed, "watch your tongue!"

"Are you… a Christian woman… going to let your stupid son and high-school dropout of a daughter insult my husband and my daughter?" Mrs. Pearl challenged Shug.

"As a Christian woman, it's time that I finally stand up for my children," Shug retorted, pointing her finger at Mrs. Pearl, Reverend Hurley, and Alspice. "Let this be the last time you, your fat ass husband, or your hussy of a daughter insult my children."

"My husband is a man of God," Mrs. Pearl said, shocked by Shug's aggression. "And if you feel that way, you and your children can walk home!"

"That's fine with us!" Shug replied.

"Pearl… you shouldn't have talked about Miss Shug and her children that way," her sister, Portia, chimed. "Pookie only did what you should've done a long time ago. Stand up to your rat of a husband!"

"Portia is right," Priscilla agreed, echoing her twin sister.

"You two old maids need to stay the hell out of me and my wife's business!" Reverend Hurley shouted.

"Don't be rude to my sisters," Tyrone, Jr. intervened, pushing his way through the crowd to confront his brother-in-law. He then pointed his manicured fingernails in Reverend Hurley's face. "After my father died—you took over his farm, his house, and his church! And we want them all back!"

"I bet my daddy is turning over in his grave," Portia added. "He probably won't ever rest in peace until we get rid of you, Horace!"

"If your daddy is turning over in his grave, it's because he has four girls," Reverend Hurley responded, smirking at his insult at Tyrone.

"You filthy skirt chaser!" Portia exclaimed. "What are you trying to imply about our father?"

"Ask your brother, Tyrone," Reverend Hurley suggested.

"Tyrone… what's Horace trying to say?" Priscilla asked. "Did our father have a fourth daughter that we don't know about?"

"Horace is a lying piece of shit," Tyrone said, cowering away from the subject.

Tyrone was not yet ready to divulge to his old-fashioned twin sisters what he had previously admitted to Mrs. Pearl. They were much too religious and judgmental to accept the truth about his sexuality.

"Horace… leave Tyrone alone," Mrs. Pearl said, removing food from her dress with a plastic fork. She then turned to Shug and apologetically said, "Forget what I said about y'all walking home. Horace didn't mean what he said, either. We've been friends too long to let a little disagreement come between us."

"A little disagreement," Reverend Hurley said, pointing at Shug. "That woman and her dumb children aren't getting back in my car until they apologize to us in front of the whole congregation!"

"What about me?" Alspice asked. "I deserve an apology, too!"

"You're right," Reverend Hurley agreed, acknowledging his daughter's request. "Not until they apologize to me, my wife, and daughter in front of our parishioners."

"Hell will freeze before…" Pookie said, boldly.

"You better wash that girl's mouth out with soap," Reverend Hurley interrupted before Pookie could complete her sentence. He and Alspice then stepped on the food and paper plate covered ground as they hurried away in anger. Before getting into his station wagon, Reverend Hurley demanded, “Pearl, come on! Let’s go home!”

“Go on home with your husband,” Shug said to a hesitant Mrs. Pearl.

“Tyrone, will you take Shug and her kids home?” Mrs. Pearl asked, trying to mend their friendship.

“Don’t worry, Pearl,” Tyrone responded. “We’ll see that they get home safely.”

“Be ready to apologize,” Reverend Hurley shouted as Mrs. Pearl finally got into the car and he drove away.

“When hell freezes over,” Pookie silently repeated, looking around for Johnny who was nowhere in sight.

When the circus was over, the crowd quickly dispersed due to another unrelated fight inside the church.

The Hurley’s, McAdoo’s, and Featherstone’s had now aired their dirty laundry for the whole congregation to hear, reigniting the parishioners discussion on whether to oust Reverend Hurley or not.

"We better get going," Brother Tyrone suggested. He and Priscilla began to help Shug get June Bug prepared for the short ride home.

"Wait," Portia said. "I left my new hat in the basement!"

"Trust me… you don't want to go in that basement," Tyrone said, grabbing onto Portia's arm to prevent her from going.

"Why?" Portia asked, pulling away from her brother.

"While we were out here being childish, the children were having a food fight in the basement. It's a big mess down there!"

"Did they destroy my beautiful, expensive hat?"

"Well… big sister, consider that hat a loss," Tyrone replied, regretfully.

"I'll buy you another one," Priscilla said, consoling her sister. "But, who's going to clean up the mess?"

"Alma and Paul said they would come back tomorrow and take care of it," Tyrone answered. "It looks like it's going to storm. We better get out of here."

No one wanted to make the first move toward Tyrone's pink Oldsmobile. Everybody remained in the same spot as though they were glued to the ground. Portia and Priscilla held hands while Tyrone ran his manicured nails through his long processed hair. He mumbled some curse words when he found a few stains on his white linen suit.

June Bug laid his head in Shug's lap. He began to whine due to a severe toothache that was ailing him. During all of the bickering, he had secretly eaten most of the coconut cake that had fallen on the ground.

As Pookie was thinking that Johnny was a coward for disappearing, she suddenly saw him driving toward the church in Mr. Bill's red truck. He had miraculously become Pookie's hero once again. She was not only ecstatic to see him, but glad to avoid having to ride home with Tyrone and his holier-than-thou sisters, Portia and Priscilla. From the look on Shug's face, she was also happy to see Johnny because in all honesty, she did not want to ride with the stuffy Featherstone's either.

Johnny got out of the truck and spoke to everyone before announcing that he would drive the McAdoo's home. That was good news to the Featherstones who really did not want the ungodly Pookie or the unruly June Bug in their car either.

Johnny helped Shug and June Bug into the cab of the truck. There was not enough room for the four of them inside the small vehicle. Pookie would have to sit in the bed of the truck. She, wearing a skirt and heels, was very embarrassed when Johnny helped her climb into the back and sit on the rusty floor. However, there was no other alternative. Shug was not going to let her walk and neither was she going to get dropped off at home first, allowing Johnny to return unsupervised for Pookie.

Pookie sat as low as she could, hoping no one would see her riding in the back of Mr. Bill's old truck. The short ride seemed like an eternity. When Johnny arrived at their house, he parked near the front door. He helped Shug get a sleepy June Bug up the stoop, onto the porch, and into the house.

This left Pookie waiting on Johnny to help her get out of the truck. Still feeling humiliated, Pookie decided to climb down on her own in an attempt to avoid Johnny getting another look up her dress.

"I was going to help you," Johnny said to Pookie as she climbed out the truck. "June Bug wouldn't let Miss Shug take him to his room, so I helped her."

"I'm glad you came back to get us."

"I hope you didn't think I was some coward that

deserted you."

"Well…."

Before Pookie could finish her statement, Shug came to the door and said, "Thanks for all of your help, Johnny."

"You're most welcome, Miss Shug," Johnny answered, hoping Shug's compliment would somehow allow him to get closer to Pookie.

"If it's too late when Pookie gets off of work tomorrow, will you see to it that she gets home safely?" Shug asked, reluctantly. "My car is still down."

"Be glad to, Miss Shug," Johnny said, glancing at Pookie.

"Pookie, come on in the house," Shug requested. "Tomorrow is the first day on your new job. You need to be well-rested."

"See you tomorrow, Pookie," Johnny said, as he turned to leave.

"Bye," Pookie responded, waiting until Johnny was almost out of her sight before going into the house.

On the way to her room, Pookie stopped by June

Bug's bedroom. Shug was sitting on the edge of his bed, eating a piece of chicken as she waited for him to eventually fall asleep. From all of the cake he had eaten, June Bug not only had a toothache, but also a stomachache. He desperately needed to see a dentist, but it would be two more weeks before Shug had enough money to take him. Normally, she would ask Reverend Hurley for a loan. But after their confrontation, there was no way she could muster up the courage to do so.

Attempting to alleviate his pain, Shug held a paper cup filled with salty water to June Bug's mouth and told him to gargle. He spat on the floor that which he refused to gargle.

Shug crumbled the cup in her hand. She laid it on his bedside table next to the plate of her leftover chicken. Before pulling his blanket around his bony body and gigantic head, she took a piece of used tissue and wiped away the saliva that ran from the corner of his mouth and down the stringy hairs on his elongated chin.

Shug was exhausted and worried. With the tissue still in her hand and without speaking, she passed by Pookie, as if she were invisible, and went to her room. Pookie followed Shug to their room, which was lit only by the neighborhood street posts.

Before getting into bed and facing the wall, Shug dropped the soiled tissue on her junky and dusty dresser. Even though their tiny room was hot and humid, Shug pulled the sheets tightly around her shoulders as if she were freezing cold or as if she were afraid that someone would come in, during the night, and harm her while she slept. Everything in the room became still, except for the used tissue that held June Bug's saliva. The faintest breeze, coming through the barely open window, fluttered the tissue back and forth. Through the dimness, it looked like a wounded butterfly trying to take flight.

"Are you angry with me?" Pookie asked.

"Angry with you about what?"

"About what I said to Reverend Hurley."

"No, I'm not. Horace is not the man of God that I thought he was."

"I'm glad you're not mad at me."

"Are you coming to bed?"

"Can I sit on the stoop for a while?"

"Don't sit out there too long. Make sure the door is closed and locked when you come back inside."

"Yes, ma'am," Pookie said, quietly exiting the room.

Pookie tucked her skirt around her legs and sat on the stoop. Alone, with only the typical noises emitting through her slummy neighborhood, she reminisced about the day's events.

Some of Pookie's recollections saddened her while others made her smile. She was disappointed that her and Alspice's argument caused friction between Shug and her good friend, Mrs. Pearl. Nevertheless, thoughts of Johnny made her smile.

"What if Johnny and I leave Alabaster, get married, and become rich and famous stars? We could build a beautiful home, big enough for Shug and June Bug to live with us. I don't think Johnny would mind. He must like June Bug because he lets him wear his precious blue cap."

Pookie continued to think to herself. "I hope my dreams come to pass sooner than later. I've heard kids tease June Bug, claiming folks with his condition don't live long. Shug told me not to listen to them because only God knows the time and the hour of the coming of the Lord. But if death really comes like a thief in the night, how much longer do I have with my sweet brother or for that matter, my dear mother?"

Three people walking toward her house took Pookie's attention away from her thoughts. Pookie could barely see the three individuals due to the neighborhood gangs shooting out most of the streetlights, except for a few that remained intact. The shadowy silhouettes of two adults and a crying child, attempting to keep up with the adults, seemed familiar. Upon them getting closer, Pookie recognized one of the adults as Tilly and the child as her four-year-old daughter, Tammie Sue.

"Good evening, Miss Tilly," Pookie said, loudly. "You and Tammy Sue are out mighty late."

Tilly stopped walking when she heard Pookie's voice, which caused Tammy Sue to bump into her and fall on the ground. In an attempt to hide his identity from Pookie, the unidentified man quickly fled in the opposite direction.

Tilly shouted, "Run on home to your naïve wife… you low-down son-of-a-bitch," at the fleeing man. She then demanded that Tammy Sue get up and stop her crying. The visibly unkempt and exhausted, yet obedient, toddler did as she was instructed.

"Shug… is that you?" Tilly asked.

"No, ma'am. It's me, Pookie."

"Pookie McAdoo?"

"Yes, ma'am."

"Where's your mama?"

"She's in the house, asleep."

"Maybe you should take Tammy Sue home," Pookie suggested, feeling sorry for the small child. "She looks sleepy."

"I'm having too much trouble carrying this to carry a heavy child," Tilly said, raising a pint of whiskey concealed in a brown paper bag.

"Pookie… are you still there?"

"Yes, ma'am?"

"Get your cute little ass in the house," Tilly said, stumbling as she and Tammy Sue continued on their way. "You can't handle these street hoodlums like I can."

Tilly picked up Tammy Sue, dressed only in a soiled diaper and no shoes, and carried her down the littered street. Pookie watched them until they walked past the last functioning light post.

Pookie eventually dozed off to sleep, leaning her head against the wall of the porch. The whistles of the northern bound train and the licks of a small brown puppy awakened her early the next morning. She could not fathom that she had fallen asleep outside in her dangerous and dilapidated neighborhood. Luckily—the drunkards, druggies, and gangs had not noticed her as they roamed throughout the night. Shug would kill her if she knew.

Pookie rubbed the friendly dog on his head. She had always wanted a puppy of her own, but Shug said they could not afford to feed another mouth.

The emaciated dog was hungry and his brown eyes were caked with crusty discharge. Although Shug had always warned Pookie against feeding stray cats and dogs, claiming they would not leave, the dog's mirthful personality instantaneously won Pookie over.

Pookie remembered the scraps of chicken that Shug had left on June Bug's bedside table. She decided to give them to the stray dog.

Leaving the dog on the stoop, Pookie took off her shoes and tiptoed into June Bug's room. As usual, he had kicked his covers onto the floor. Pookie could not take the chance of awakening him or Shug, so she quickly grabbed the scraps of chicken and hurried back to the waiting dog.

Pookie threw the scraps out into the yard. The dog ran down the stoop and began to devour them. She was hoping that the dog, whose ribs protruded through its sides, would be gone by the time she left for her new job at Bill's Hardware.

Pookie then went to her room and got into bed with Shug, who was still sound asleep.

CHAPTER 5

June Bug's giggling awoke Shug and Pookie. Since he had been crying out in pain earlier, they were surprised to hear happy noises coming from his bedroom. As Shug went to check on her son, she noticed streaks of daylight coming through the front door. Her first thought was that Pookie might have forgotten to close the door before going to bed.

As she contemplated the possibility that it could also mean that an intruder could be in the house, Shug feared for her family's safety. She hurried back to her room and retrieved a hammer that she kept under her bed for protection.

She whispered in Pookie's ear, telling her that the front was open and that someone might be in the house. Shug was planning to fight off the attacker while Pookie led June Bug away from harm. Shug raised the hammer into the air and charged head first down the hallway.

Pookie then dashed by Shug, tightly holding June Bug's plastic bat and a broomstick. There was no way that she was going to abandon Shug. She had decided to either fight saving her family or to die trying.

Pookie, followed closely by Shug, ran into June Bug's room. They did not find an intruder. Instead they saw a small brown puppy on his bed. June Bug was giggling and rubbing the dog's head as it licked him all over his face. Pookie recognized the stray dog as the one she had fed straps of chicken. She assumed that the front door must not have been closed all the way when she came inside. The dog had obviously pushed the front door open and found his way into June Bug's room.

Pookie knew she would be in a lot of trouble if Shug found out how the dog got into the house. She quickly decided to be honest and face her punishment. Pookie eased the hammer out of Shug's hand and slid it, along with the broomstick, underneath June Bug's bed.

"Look at June Bug," Shug said, smiling. "He likes that puppy."

"Can we keep her?"

"It's a he… and no… we can't."

"Why not?"

"His name is Brownie and he belongs to Mr. Bill's wife, Barbara."

"Are you sure that dog belongs to Mrs. Roberson?" Pookie asked, pointing to the dog as it showered June Bug with kisses.

"Brownie runs to meet me every time I go to work at Mrs. Roberson's house. He's been missing for over a week."

"I guess that's why he was so hungry."

"How did you know he was hungry?"

"I...."

"I don't even want to know," Shug interrupted. "When you go to work today, tell Mr. Bill that his wife's dog is at our house."

"If it's okay with Mrs. Roberson, can we keep Brownie?"

"No!"

"Look how happy he makes June Bug."

"Barbara loves her dog. She's been looking everywhere for him."

"Can we ask her if she's willing to give Brownie to us?"

"We can't afford a dog."

"But...."

"But nothing," Shug responded. "Let go of the dog, June Bug! After you eat breakfast, you and Brownie can play outside."

"I can...."

"I don't want to hear anything else about that dog," Shug declared. "Pookie... fix your brother a bowl of oatmeal!"

"Yes, ma'am."

Pookie went into the kitchen. She searched the cabinets for the box of instant oatmeal before remembering that Shug kept it in the refrigerator to prevent rats from chewing through it. The refrigerator was completely empty, except for the box of oatmeal and a half-gallon of milk, which nobody yet realized was spoiled.

Pookie checked to see if Shug was on her way into the kitchen. When she saw that the coast was clear, she drank the milk directly from the container. Upon tasting the sourness, Pookie held the milk in her mouth to keep from swallowing. She spat it into the kitchen sink of dirty dishes and put the container back in the refrigerator.

Shug and June Bug then came into the kitchen with Brownie, trotting in behind them before lying on the floor. Shug told June Bug to be a good boy and to eat all of his oatmeal while she went to pickup trash from the yard.

Pookie lit the gas stove and filled the kettle with water. She then set the kettle over the flames. As the water boiled, she reached to get a bowl. When she opened the cabinet, a rat jumped out. The vermin fell into the large, cast iron skillet of chicken grease that had been left on top of the stove. Leaving its foot and tail prints in the congealed fat, it scrambled to the floor and fled into a hole in the wall.

Pookie got the bowl, stained with blackberry juice, and poured hot water and oatmeal into it. She stirred the mixture with the cleanest spoon that she could find among the dirty dishes in the sink. Pookie set the bland porridge and the spoon on the table so that June Bug could eat. Instead, he dumped the oatmeal on the floor. Brownie immediately gobbled up the warm cereal.

Not to be outdone, Pookie made another bowl and spoon-fed it to June Bug. Afterwards, she cleaned his sticky face and called for Shug to come and get him and Brownie.

June Bug began to fiddle with the zipper of his pants because he needed to use the bathroom. However, before Shug could take him, he unzipped his pants and urinated on the kitchen floor. Pookie pretended not to look until Shug had him presentable. As Shug mopped up the ammonia-smelling urine, she chatted with Pookie.

"Pookie... you don't want to be late for your first day to work."

"Can I tell Mr. Bill about Brownie tomorrow?"

"I guess so. You know my car is down so you'll have to walk home. Don't talk to any strangers or accept any rides from anyone."

"I promise."

On her way to Bill's Hardware, Pookie hastened through her neighborhood. She remembered Shug and Tilly's warning about the dangers of a young girl walking alone, especially in an area like hers.

The houses were unkempt and the yards were littered with trash. The deserted, boarded-up buildings were primarily used by drug dealers to sell narcotics or by drug users to snort cocaine and shoot-up heroin. Criminals preyed upon the homeless as they desperately sought a safe place to rest or sleep. Pookie had to cover her nose in order to mask the smell of dead animals, decaying near the curb. Her neighborhood had become one large cesspool of dysfunction.

Pookie ignored the whistles and catcalls from the men that stood idly against the graffiti-covered buildings. She began to walk faster through the neighborhood that she hoped to one day escape and never return to.

Pookie was almost out of breath when she finally arrived at Bill's Hardware. Mr. Bill was a very handsome man, whose gray hair was always neatly groomed. Pookie found his constant smiling extremely attractive. He would often slip Shug a few extra dollars for housekeeping or ironing when his stingy wife was not looking.

Mr. Bill told Pookie that he would be with her as soon as he finished helping the only customer who was in the store. He gave the patron a box of nails. The man tried to pay, but Mr. Bill would not accept his money. Mr. Bill waited until the man had left before he went to talk with Pookie.

From the look on his face, Pookie knew that he had bad news. Mr. Bill began to apologize, stating that he and his wife had decided that after forty-five years of running a community hardware business that they could no longer compete with the larger chains. He stated that they had reluctantly made the decision to close the store and move to Florida. He agreed to allow Pookie to work just for the day so she did not have to travel all that way in vain. Feeling sorry for her and Shug's predicament, he also offered to pay her a week's salary.

Mr. Bill then escorted Pookie into the stockroom where Johnny was taking inventory. From the smile on Johnny and Pookie's faces, Mr. Bill knew they needed no introduction. He then left the room, leaving Johnny and Pookie alone.

"Did Mr. Bill tell you the bad news about the store?"

"Yes. The news isn't going to be good for Shug either. What are you going to do for a job?"

"Remember, I have another job at Bettie's."

"Oh, yes! I forgot."

Only a few minutes had passed before Mr. Bill returned to the stockroom. He looked at the clock on the wall and realized that it was way past Johnny's quitting time. Although Johnny insisted on finishing the inventory, Mr. Bill stated that it could wait until another day. Reluctantly, Johnny handed the pencil and pad to him.

"Johnny, do you remember my wife's brown dog?" Mr. Bill asked.

"Yes, sir… I do."

"He strayed away from our house about a week ago. On your way home, please keep an eye out for him."

"I certainly will, Mr. Bill."

"Thanks, Johnny."

"I promised Miss Shug that I would make sure that Pookie got home safely," Johnny said, justifying why he was still hanging around the store.

"Well in that case… you can go ahead and take the day off Pookie," Mr. Bill said, smiling.

"Thanks, Mr. Bill," Pookie replied, smiling back.

"I want to extend my apologies to you and Shug again. I know you were depending on this job."

"That's very kind of you."

"And Pookie… please help Johnny search for dog."

"I'll be glad to, Mr. Bill."

Johnny and Pookie then left the store walking. She was happy to spend as much time as she could in his presence.

"It's early," Johnny said, looking down at his watch. "Let's go by my house so you can meet my uncle. He can help you get another job."

"Help me get another job where?"

"At Bettie's Blues Barn. Since you don't have the job at Bill's Hardware anymore, what are you going to do? Soon… Shug will no longer have her ironing or housekeeping money either."

"I don't know what we're going to do, but Shug would kill me if I got a job at Bettie's."

"I thought becoming a singer was a dream of yours?"

"It is, but…."

"Well… let me know what you decide. Are you going to my house with me to meet my uncle?"

"What about the dog?"

"What dog?"

"Mrs. Roberson's dog."

"Forget about that dog for now."

"I can't because…."

"Because what?"

"Because Brownie is at my house with June Bug."

"Then let June Bug keep him."

"What about Mrs. Roberson?"

"Forget Mrs. Roberson," Johnny replied, frustrated with the childish Pookie.

Johnny held Pookie's hand as he led her through his neat, quiet neighborhood. It was a drastic difference from hers. He pointed to a brick house where the lawn was neatly trimmed and flowers were planted in the garden.

"That's where I live."

"Wow," Pookie said, comparing Johnny's beautiful house to hers. "You weren't lying when you said that you lived close to my church."

"Let's go inside and meet my uncle."

"Maybe some other time."

"What about tomorrow?"

"I'll think about it," Pookie replied, shrugging her shoulders.

Johnny and Pookie continued to walk past his house and toward Mount Holy. They then saw Reverend Hurley driving his station wagon with a sinister smile on his wrinkled face. He veered his car in the direction of Pookie and Johnny, almost hitting them. To keep from being run over, they both jumped into a ditch. Although Reverend Hurley had seen them fall to the ground, he did not stop. He sped down the road, leaving Pookie and Johnny in shock. After Johnny helped Pookie out of the ditch, he saw that her left knee was bleeding through her jeans.

"Are you hurt?" Johnny asked as he quickly looked to see if Reverend Hurley was making a U-turn in an attempt to run them over again.

"I hurt my knee."

"Did you see the look on that evil man's face?"

"Yes," Pookie said, still shaken. "Why did he do that to us?"

"I have no idea. Only hate would make someone do what he just did."

"I'm scared!"

"I'll protect you. Come on… let me get you home before he comes back."

When Pookie arrived home, she and Johnny could hear June Bug crying. They immediately went to his room. June Bug was lying on his bed as Shug sat in a chair, trying to console him. He had a rag wrapped around his swollen jaw.

"What's wrong with June Bug?" Pookie asked.

"He has a real bad toothache," Shug replied, holding June Bug's hand. "I gave him a strong sedative. He'll be asleep soon. Hopefully, he'll sleep through the night and into the early morning."

"Pookie told me that Mrs. Roberson's dog was at your house," Johnny said.

"Where's Brownie?" Pookie asked, looking around June Bug's room.

"Mrs. Roberson took him back with her." Shug said.

"How did she know he was here?" Pookie asked,

disappointed that Brownie was gone.

"She saw him when she brought some clothes over for me to iron. Brownie must have recognized the sound of her car because he came running out of the house."

"I'm sure that made June Bug very sad," Pookie replied.

"She also told me the bad news about Bill's Hardware closing and them moving to Florida," Shug said in a stressful voice.

"Miss Shug… June Bug has gone to sleep," Johnny said, interrupting their conversation.

"Let's go into the kitchen so we don't wake him," Shug suggested.

They quietly left June Bug's room and went into the kitchen, which was usually immaculate. The sink was free of dirty dishes and the stove was wiped clean. The floor was shining and the refrigerator no longer held the expired milk carton. Pookie knew that Shug must have been extremely burdened because that was the only time that she cleaned with such diligence. Perhaps, Shug thought that by cleaning up her house, to the extent she had, that her life's troubles would also become organized. But that was just wishful thinking. Both Pookie and Shug knew the depth of their dire dilemma could not be solved with a mop and a bucket of bleach.

“Did you hurt your knee?” Shug asked, looking down at the bloody stain on Pookie’s jeans.

“Yes, ma’am.”

“How?”

“I hurt it when Johnny and I had to jump into a ditch.”

“Why did y’all have to jump in a ditch?”

“Reverend Hurley tried to hit us with his station wagon.”

“If we hadn’t jumped out of the way when we did, he most certainly would’ve,” Johnny added.

“Johnny, did you get hurt?” Shug inquired.

“No, ma’am,” Johnny replied, adjusting his blue cap.

“Pookie… put some alcohol on your knee before it gets infected,” Shug said.

"It's getting late," Johnny said. "Can I use your telephone? I need to call someone to give me a ride to Bettie's?"

"I got behind on my bill," Shug replied, embarrassed. "My telephone is disconnected."

"I'll stop down the street at a telephone booth," Johnny said.

"Be careful," Pookie said, opening the empty refrigerator before quickly closing it back.

"I will," Johnny responded. "Tomorrow… I'll ask Mr. Bill to see if his wife will let June Bug have Brownie."

"Thanks," Shug responded, having grown attached to the small dog.

Pookie walked Johnny to the door. She watched him walk away until he was completely out of sight. She then went back into the kitchen where Shug was holding a glass of water and two of June Bug's pain pills.

"I'm beginning to like that boy," Shug admitted. "Here… take these two pills and drink this water."

"For what?" Pookie asked.

"They will keep your knee from getting infected."

"But, you'll need them for June Bug's toothache."

"I have some more."

"How are we going to get money to pull his teeth?"

"I'll get the money, somehow… someway."

"If I apologize to Reverend Hurley and his family, he'd let you borrow some money."

"When hell freezes over!" Shug exclaimed. "Now… I'm going to bed. God knows I need the rest."

Left in the kitchen alone, Pookie swallowed the two pills. She sat at the table, rolled up the leg of her jeans, and poured a few drops of alcohol on her superficial wound. It stung for a few seconds, but not nearly as much as the sting of losing her job. She felt horrible that she was unable to monetarily help Shug. To compound matters, Shug would soon be jobless as well.

Until they could do better, Pookie reasoned that the only logical thing to do was to apologize to Reverend Hurley. That would set the stage for Shug to be able to borrow some money from him.

Pookie then remembered that Reverend Hurley usually spent late evenings at Mount Holy, working with his secretary or preparing his sermons. She decided that since Shug was sound asleep that she would go to the church and repent her sins to the false prophet, Reverend Hurley.

However, the medicine that Pookie had taken started to make her drowsy. It seemed like the pills Shug had given her were more similar to sleeping pills than antibiotics to ward off an infection.

She rested her head on the table. Pookie's quick nap, nevertheless, turned into a deep slumber. She was awakened hours later by the sounds of someone opening and closing the front door. Still somewhat groggy, Pookie could not decipher if it was late at night or early in the morning.

The darkness hampered her vision. Dazed, she thought she saw someone walking down the hall towards June Bug's bedroom. Pookie shook her head to make sure that she was not dreaming. Could there be a real intruder in their house this time?

Pookie quietly removed her shoes before tiptoeing down the hallway. Her heart was pounding against her chest. She then glanced into June Bug's room. His nightlight was on and he was under the covers. When Pookie saw that her brother was safe, she continued to her and Shug's bedroom.

When she peered inside, she realized that there was no intruder. It was only Shug—fully dressed in a black long-sleeved shirt, black pants, and a pair of old tennis shoes. Small twigs and leaves clung to the back of her shirt. In hindsight, Pookie surmised that while she slept, Shug must have left the house and had just returned. Bewildered, because her mother had never done such a thing, Pookie pondered where she could have possibly been.

To keep Shug from noticing her, she crept back into the kitchen. She looked at the clock and saw that it was three-thirty in the morning. After a few moments, Pookie returned to their room. Shug was now dressed in her nightgown, staring wide-eyed at the ceiling.

"Did I wake you?" Pookie asked, already knowing the answer to her question.

"No."

"Are you worried about not having enough money to pay next month's bills?"

"Not anymore."

"Why not?"

"Remind me to get those cobwebs off of the ceiling," Shug responded, ignoring Pookie's inquiry.

"What cobwebs? I don't see any."

"They're up there," Shug said, turning on her side with her back to Pookie. "You don't have to see everything to know it's there. Sometimes… you just know."

In the stillness of the wee hours of the morning, Pookie then took off her bloodstained jeans and her grass-stained top. In only her panties and bra, she climbed into bed next to Shug.

Thoughts of the day's events clouded her mind. She was stressed beyond her years. "What will we do now that I've lost my job? Maybe if I had gone to meet Johnny's uncle, we would've avoided seeing Reverend Hurley? Why did he try to run us over with his car? Where on earth could Shug have been?"

She suddenly heard the sad wails of a distant train calling out to her.

"One day… I'm going to ride that train," Pookie whispered.

"What did you say?"

“Just thinking out loud.”

“About what?”

“Nothing important.”

CHAPTER 6

Pookie awaken to a note from Shug on her pillow. It read, "Taking June Bug to the dentist. Be back soon."

Since she was home alone, Pookie used it as an opportunity to lounge in bed for a while longer. She laid on her back and looked at the ceiling, still unable to see any cobwebs.

For once, she had the house all to herself. She was enjoying her solitude until there was a knock at the front door. Pookie remained quiet, assuming Jehovah Witnesses were passing out pamphlets. She then heard Johnny calling her name.

Hearing his voice made Pookie's heart flutter. She jumped out of bed and ran into the bathroom. She got dressed in the cleanest of her dirty jeans and shirts. She then combed her hair with Shug's broken-tooth comb.

Pookie ran into the living room and peeped out of the window. Johnny, driving Mr. Bill's truck, had Brownie with him. When he saw Pookie glancing at him, he beckoned for her to open the door. However, Pookie first cupped her hands and blew into them to test the freshness of her breath.

“Look who I have with me.”

“How did you get Brownie back?”

“When I told Mr. Bill how June Bug loved Brownie, he went to his house and got him for me to bring back.”

“Mr. Bill is such a nice man.”

“Well… can we come in?”

“Brownie can, but you can’t.”

“Why not?”

“Shug and June Bug aren’t home.”

“I know. I saw them pass by in a taxi.”

“If you knew Shug wasn’t home, why did you ask to come inside?”

“Just to see what you would say.”

“Well… now you know.”

"I have Mr. Bill's truck. He told me that I could keep it for the rest of the day. Want to go for a ride?"

Assuming that Shug would be gone for most of the day, Pookie accepted Johnny's invitation. She let Brownie inside the house and locked the door. Forgetting about her sloppy appearance, she then left with Johnny.

They rode past Mount Holy where she was reminded of her and Johnny's encounter with Reverend Hurley. She was also reminded of the stupid mistake she would have made if she had gone to beg him for forgiveness instead of falling asleep.

"After you left my house, did you see Reverend Hurley last night?"

"On my way home from Bettie's, around three o'clock in the morning, I saw his station wagon parked behind the church."

"That was mighty late for him to be pastoring. Don't you think?"

"He was probably ministering to one of his many secretaries."

"Where are we going?"

"We're going to my house. I want you to meet my uncle, Toby."

"I can't go to your house! I shouldn't even be riding with you! Shug is going to kill me!"

"She won't find out. Besides… I got a feeling that you and my uncle will become the best of friends."

"But…."

"Relax, you're with me. I'm the person who saved you from being run over by Reverend Hurley... remember?"

"Okay, but we can't stay long."

"I promise."

Johnny unlocked the door to his modest brick home. As they walked down the dark hallway, Pookie could barely see her feet. She began to wonder if she had trusted Johnny a little too much. That was until he took her into the living room and turned on the lights. He then raised the window shades. The bright lights illuminated the room and its décor. A blue leather sofa, loveseat, and matching recliner encircled a beige shag carpet. Photos of famous musicians—such as Ray Charles, Aretha Franklin, Chuck Berry, Al Green, Fats Domino, Etta James,

Gladys Knight and the Pips, and even one of Elvis Presley—hung on the walls.

A tall handsome man, wearing dark sunglasses, sat in the recliner. Pookie thought he was dead because he did not acknowledge their presence until Johnny began to talk.

"Uncle Toby, I want you to meet Pookie McAdoo," Johnny said, escorting her closer to the man's chair.

"Glad to meet you, Pookie," Toby responded, moving towards the edge of the recliner.

"Nice to meet you, too," Pookie said, extending her hand towards Toby.

"Toby is legally blind," Johnny explained.

"My apologies," Pookie said, quickly dropping her hand to her side.

"Johnny told me you wanted to become a professional blues singer," Toby said. "That's a big challenge for a young girl like yourself."

"Yes, sir," Pookie answered.

"Then, come to Bettie's one weekend," Toby suggested. "Show us what you're made of."

"If my mama lets me," Pookie responded.

"You want me to ask her for you?" Toby asked.

"No, sir," Pookie said, noticing a van pulling into their driveway.

"Uncle Toby, your ride is here," Johnny interrupted.

"That must be Raymond, the drummer at Mount Holy," Toby surmised. "He works at the church on Sundays and will start drumming at Bettie's on the other six days."

"Really?" Johnny asked, surprised.

"I've seen him several times at Mount Holy," Pookie added. "He was playing the drums when I sung my solo last Sunday."

"Today is his first day at Bettie's," Toby responded. "I'm going to ride with him."

"I'll welcome him to the family when I get to work," Johnny said.

"Why don't you let Johnny bring you by the club tonight?" Toby inquired.

"Not tonight," Pookie responded, knowing Shug

would skin her alive.

"Just let me know when," Toby said, grinning. "You'll be my special guest."

"Thanks Mr. Toby," Pookie said.

"Just call me Toby. Any girl that put Reverend Horace Hurley in his place the way you did is always welcome at my house."

"Thanks, Toby," Pookie answered, blushing.

"I better not keep Raymond waiting," Toby said, walking toward the door to leave. "I'll see you two later."

Pookie followed Johnny and Toby to the front door. She watched as Johnny helped him get into the van. She was impressed with the charismatic Toby. She not only liked him, but also felt extremely comfortable in his home.

Pookie's comfort was, however, short lived when Reverend Hurley sped by Johnny's house in his station wagon. Before she was able to step away from the door, he slowed down and looked directly at her. As Raymond and Toby backed out of the driveway, he superficially waved although secretly looking in her direction. Reverend Hurley and Pookie's eyes locked, for what seemed like an eternity, before he promptly sped away. She was certain that he would tell Shug that she had been at Johnny's house without her permission.

"Johnny, Reverend Hurley just passed by your house."

"Yeah… I saw him."

"He gave me the nastiest look. I'm sure he's going to tell Shug that I was here."

"Don't worry."

"I really do hate that man!"

"When it comes to hating Reverend Hurley, you're certainly not the only one."

"Go inside the house and I'll be in shortly. I'm going to park the truck in the back yard so if he drives by again, he'll think we're gone.

"Johnny, I better get home."

"Stay just a little while longer," Johnny pleaded. "Then I'll take you home."

As Johnny moved the truck, Pookie went inside

the house. She wanted to wait for him instead of walking uninvited around his house. However, she had to use the bathroom. Passing by two bedrooms, Pookie finally found it. She fumbled for the light switch before turning it on. She then closed the door behind her, pulled down her jeans, set down on the cool toilet seat, and urinated.

The bathroom floor was cleaner than Pookie's kitchen floor. The commode was cleaner than her kitchen sink. Unlike at her and Shug's house, their bathtub was not being used to store dirty clothes.

Pookie made sure she did not leave any urine on their white commode. She washed her hands and dried them on one of the neatly folded towels.

She looked into the mirror that hung on the back of the door. Her curly hair, cropped closely to her large head, made her look boyish and her breasts were the size of golf balls. The hair under her armpits was as bushy as her pubic hair. Pookie saw nothing about herself that she liked. She closed her eyes and felt her breasts while wishing they were as voluptuous as Alspice's.

Pookie moved her hands down her chest towards her navel and then to her vagina. Her own touches made her feel aroused. She wondered what it would be like to lose her virginity. Engrossed in her own pleasure, she did not notice that Johnny had come into the bathroom until he whispered her name.

He then came in, closing the door behind him. He stood next to her and placed his hand on top of hers. Pookie's eyes remained closed as Johnny now lead both of their hands over her private parts. Her body was begging for his attention and he was more than prepared to answer her pleas.

He turned Pookie to face him. She—inexperienced, though ready to learn—rubbed his smooth chest. He then passionately kissed her, sticking his tongue far down her throat. Like a desert snake looking for a cool place to hide, Johnny's firm penis found its way into Pookie's innocence.

Afterward, Johnny left Pookie to her privacy. She again urinated, dropping the blood and semen-stained tissue into the commode. Pookie watched the tissue flush out of sight, carrying her innocence with it. As her concupiscent desires subsided, the realization of losing her virginity hit her like a ton of bricks. She remembered what Shug had said about, "Whatever mistakes you make will ride your behind for the rest of your life." If Shug were right, Pookie's derriere would have a lot to carry.

Pookie left the bathroom and went into Johnny's bedroom. He was already dressed and sitting at the foot of the bed. His blue cap was pulled tightly down on his head.

"I think I should go home now," Pookie declared.

"I agree. I'll pull the truck around and honk for you to come out."

However, their plans were suddenly spoiled when they heard a car pulling into the driveway. Johnny glanced out of the window.

"It's Miss Shug!"

"Oh my God! She's going to kill me!"

"Toby, June Bug, and Brownie are with her."

"How did they get here?"

"She's driving her Chevrolet. She must've gotten it fixed."

"What are we going to do?"

"Don't worry," Johnny assured her, locking his bedroom door. "They'll assume we're gone since they won't see the truck."

As they knelt down by the side of the bed, they heard the front door open. Shug and Toby had now come into the house.

"Shug... they're not here," Toby said, calling out to Johnny. "His truck is gone, but we can check his bedroom if you like."

"They better not be in his bedroom!"

"You don't have to worry about Johnny. He's a good fellow. He'll never harm Pookie."

Toby then tried to open Johnny's door, turning the doorknob back and forth. Upon finding it locked, he and Shug lingered near the door and chatted as Pookie and Johnny nervously listened.

"I'm sure Pookie is back home by now."

"Why would Johnny bring her to his house?"

"He wanted to show off his new girl."

"Pookie isn't Johnny's girl!"

"I can't believe that after all of these years, we run back into each other. I'm glad you stopped by Bettie's to look for Pookie."

"I'm glad I did, too. It's good to see you again."

"Let me fix you a drink."

"I can't leave June Bug and Brownie in the car too long."

"You're welcome to bring them inside."

"Another day would be better. This won't be the last time our paths cross."

"Well… is it safe to assume that since you still go by your maiden name that you never married?"

"No, unfortunately… I didn't."

"I'm sorry you were left to raise your two children alone. I'm sure that had to be difficult on you, especially caring for a retarded child like June Bug."

"It hasn't been easy, but by the grace of God… I've managed."

"Does Pookie know the name of her and June Bug's daddy?"

"No! I would never tell her! I couldn't burden my daughter with the name of that horrible man."

"Is June Bug the way he is because of your Uncle Robert?"

"Your list of questions is getting longer and longer, Toby Wilson!"

"Shug... something has been eating at my conscious for many years and I just…."

"Just what, Toby?"

"I just want to apologize for not being there for you those years ago. Believe me… with my fading eyesight, I was no help to anyone. I thought my future was hopeless until I went to Paris with Bettie and became a damn good musician. I never made it to the big time, but it paid the bills. When I returned to the states, I searched for you a long time."

"Yeah… and no one came to my rescue although they all knew what was going on."

"I hope your low-down father and uncle burn in hell for what they did to you. And if it's any consolation to you… June Bug's daddy is probably already burning in hell. I heard that he was brutally murdered not too long ago. Someone repeatedly stabbed him as he slept in his little room behind the service station where he used to work. I'm surprised you didn't hear about it. It was all over the news stations and in the newspapers. They said it was overkill the way his throat was cut from ear to ear. He was almost beheaded."

"The Bible says, 'Vengeance is mine; I will repay, saith the Lord.'"

"Give me a chance to make it up to you.

"I just can't think about all of this right now."

"You're right. I shouldn't have…."

"It's okay, Toby."

"Will you drive me back to Bettie's? You might find Pookie and Johnny there."

"Sure I'll drive you, but Pookie McAdoo better not be within a hundred feet of that place."

Johnny and Pookie emerged from the bedroom as soon as Shug and Toby drove away. They then went into the living room. Johnny peered out of the window as Pookie sat on the far end of the loveseat.

"I can't believe Shug and Toby know each other!"

"That was a surprise to me, too," Johnny agreed.

"I can't think about any of that right now! I got to make it home before Shug does!"

"What will you tell her if you don't?"

"I'll tell her that I was at Miss Tilly's house playing with Tammy Sue."

"What if she asks her to make sure that you're telling the truth?"

"Most of the time, Tilly is drunk. She wouldn't remember if I did or not."

On the ride to Pookie's house, neither Johnny nor her spoke about what happened between them in his bathroom. Pookie's mind was occupied with Shug and Toby's conversation. It made her reflect back to an encounter she had had when she, Shug, and June Bug first moved to Alabaster from a small neighboring town.

They had come with the clothes on their backs and what little things they could pack in the trunk of Shug's Chevrolet. Pookie and June Bug were sitting in the back seat as Shug drove. They were thirsty, hungry, and even with the car windows down, very hot from the July heat.

Pookie could vividly remember Shug taking the next

EXIT because the gasoline gauge was on empty. To avoid running out of gas and being stranded on the side of the road with two children, she stopped at the first service station she saw.

An old humpbacked black man, wearing a pair of greasy coveralls, sat in front of the service station on a stack of Coca-Cola crates. He slowly got up and walked over to the car. While Shug searched her purse for her last few dollars, the man stared into the backseat at Pookie and June Bug.

Without looking at him, Shug handed the man a combination of dollar bills and coins through the window. He took the money and counted it. With his back facing them, he leaned his buttocks against the car and pumped the small amount of gas into the empty tank. Shug then went inside the service station, leaving Pookie and June Bug in the car.

When the man finished pumping the gas, he poked his head inside the car and smiled at June Bug and Pookie. His teeth were badly decayed and his breath was repugnant. His smelly breath and the gas fumes nauseated Pookie to the point of nearly vomiting.

"What's your name?" the man asked Pookie.

Pookie did not answer. June Bug, who was five years older than Pookie, abruptly stopped crying.

She and June Bug then scooted over as far away from the man as their seat would allow.

"Well... I'm waiting for an answer," he again asked. "What's your name? Can you talk?"

"My name's Pookie," she answered, barely moving her lips as she stared into the strange man's protruding brown eyes. To her, June Bug and the man had a strong resemblance to one another.

"My name is Robert," the man said, turning his attention to June Bug. "Can you say R-o-b-e-r-t?" Upon seeing June Bug softly tapping Pookie on her head, he exclaimed, "Stop hitting that girl! Are you stupid?"

When the man told him to stop, June Bug started back crying. Hearing his cries, Shug hurried out of the service station. She was carrying a brown paper bag of goodies in one hand and a bottle of ice-cold cola in the other. She then paused to take a sip of her cola. The anticipation of drinking a soda caused Pookie to continuously lick her dry-parched lips.

Shug opened the car door and set the bag on the front seat. She then turned to thank the strange man for pumping her gas. However, upon their eyes meeting, his protruding eyes became larger as Shug's face turned redder than the beets she would force

June Bug to eat.

"Get the hell away from my car and my children!" Shug exclaimed in a loud voice. "I would have preferred to run out of gas than to see you!"

Shug's outburst caused other customers to stare. Pookie truly believed that if she and June Bug had not been in the car that she would have killed the man with her bare hands.

Shug then got into the car, slammed the door, and sped away. The man remained standing by the gas pump, yelling to the top of his voice.

"Lady, if you don't learn how to forgive and forget, you're going to have a long and rocky road ahead of you!"

"Go to hell," Shug screamed back.

Without taking her eyes off the highway, Shug handed Pookie and June Bug a bag of cookies and an orange soda. She did not drink the rest of her soda; she instead tossed the glass bottle out of the window. It hit the hot pavement, spewing liquid onto the road. Some of the broken glass landed in kudzu vines that grew along the roadside.

The humpbacked man's face and the sound of his

voice, coupled with the smell of his breath and his last words, would remain vividly etched into Pookie's memory. She wondered if this could possibly be the same man that Toby had asked Shug about. Could he have been her Uncle Robert? What had he done to her mother? From what, in her childhood, did she need rescuing from? What family secrets had her father and uncle forced Shug to keep?

Pookie and Johnny were relieved when they did not see Shug's car in the driveway. She hurried into the house while Johnny quickly drove away.

When Shug, June Bug, and Brownie finally returned home, Pookie was waiting on the stoop. Leaving June Bug and Brownie in the car, Shug carried two bags of groceries to the porch. She stood over Pookie until she eventually got the message to open the door so she could take the bags into the house.

"Where were you today?"

"I was at Miss Tilly's house. Does June Bug still have a toothache?"

"The dentist filled his cavities," Shug said with her hands on her hips. "Don't change the subject. I'll deal with you later. Who brought Brownie back to the house?"

"Johnny did. Mr. Bill gave him to June Bug."

"How long did he stay?"

"Just long enough to leave Brownie. Where did you get the money to take June Bug to the dentist, and fix your car, and buy all these groceries?"

"I ask the questions in this family, young lady. While I put the groceries away, I want you to go out to the car and bring June Bug and Brownie inside."

Pookie decided not to question Shug any further. Wherever Shug got the money from was her business. For once, Shug was humming a happy tune and not some sad spiritual.

Shug then stored the sugar, dried cereals, and cookies in the cupboard. She set the ice cream and meat into the freezer and vegetables and milk into the refrigerator. Afterwards, she began peeling potatoes for dinner.

When Pookie went out to the car, June Bug had a surprise waiting for her. He, Brownie, and the entire backseat were covered in chocolate icing and the crumbs from a cake that Shug had accidently left on the front seat.

Pookie let Brownie out of the car, but left June Bug

sitting there. She went back into the house to get a bath cloth and a pan of warm water.

"Where are you going with my pan and dishtowel?"

"I'm going to clean June Bug's face and hands. You forgot the chocolate cake?"

"June Bug got into my cake?"

"Yes, ma'am! It's all over the place."

"I'll go and help you."

"Are you going to fuss at him?"

"No. Every once in a while… everyone deserves to have his cake and eat it too. This is June Bug's day. One day you'll have yours."

Shug's statement made Pookie flashback to her sexual tryst with Johnny. She wondered if she had already eaten her cake and if so, at what price. Moreover, she and Johnny did not use any protection. The last thing she needed was a baby to destroy her life's dream of becoming famous. She certainly did not want to have a child with June Bug's condition either.

When she and Shug returned to the car, June Bug

and Brownie were gone. All that remained were his chocolate-covered clothes, lying on the car seat.

"Where did June Bug go?" Shug inquired.

"I don't know!"

"I hope that dog didn't lead June Bug towards the highway!"

"Maybe he's at Mr. Jesse's house."

"Get in the car and help me find him! I don't want my son wandering around this neighborhood, getting beat up by those gang members!"

Their first stop was at Mr. Jesse's house. Pookie hesitantly waited in the car as Shug attempted to knock on his door. His gate, however, was bolted with a chain and padlock. Realizing that there was no other way that the illogical June Bug could have gotten through the fence, Shug and Pookie continued to drive through the neighborhood. Although many of the residents had lived there for years, they did not even know their names.

Shug stopped when she saw two men leaning against a junk car, drinking beer. From the window, she asked them if they had seen June Bug.

"Sir," Shug called.

"What's on your mind, lady?" one of the men asked.

"Did either of you see a half-naked young man and a brown dog? He's retarded and may be in danger."

"We're not young and retarded," the other man said, groping his crotch. "But, we sure can get naked if that's what you're into."

"He's my son," Shug said, ignoring the man's rude comments.

"Look at the hardware on that man," one of them said as he pointed to and laughed at June Bug who suddenly came running down the street. His large penis moved back and forth like a pendulum on a grandfather clock. As June Bug wobbled closer to Shug's car, the other man exclaimed, "My cock used to be that big until I drank it to a shrimp!"

Except for his socks, June Bug was naked. He was frightened and desperately trying to escape from Tilly who was staggering behind him.

Tilly's blouse was unbuttoned, exposing her red bra. Her dingy white slip hung far below her faded yellow skirt. She was carrying June Bug's high top tennis shoes in one hand and a bottle of whiskey in the other. Brownie tried to hinder her pursuit of June Bug by barking and nipping at her feet.

"What's the matter, retard?" one of the men asked, taunting the petrified June Bug. "You don't want Miss Tilly's poontang? Take it from us, she's good!"

"You should be ashamed of yourself, Tilly!" Shug said, jumping out of the car in defense of June Bug as Pookie followed.

When Tilly saw Shug, she stopped chasing June Bug and stood in the middle of the street. Brownie continued to bark and bite at her feet. She tried to shoo him away with her half-empty whiskey bottle, but to no avail.

June Bug was elated to see Shug. He ran and tightly hugged her.

"You better keep that cock-sucking idiot away from my house or I'm going to kill him!" Tilly demanded.

"Don't give my son a bad name, Tilly!" Shug shouted. "He's a good man that just happens to have the mind of a child. June Bug has always looked to you and your house as a place of safety. And look at you standing there filthy drunk, disrespecting him."

"His mind may be that of a child, but not that long penis between his legs," Tilly responded, losing her footing. "I meant what I said! June Bug is a cock-sucker."

Shug realized that it was fruitless to quarrel with the intoxicated, foul-mouthed Tilly. Leaving his shoes for Tilly to keep, Shug helped June Bug get into the car while Pookie picked up Brownie. Shug was preparing to drive away when Tilly called her name.

"Shug… wait," Tilly said, hurrying to stand next to Shug's window. She held onto the car's door in an attempt to keep her from driving away. "Shug… when are you coming to visit me?"

"What's happened to you, Tilly?" Shug asked, ignoring Tilly's question. "You didn't use to be like this. We used to be good friends. We went to the same church and did everything together. Now… you've lost all of your dignity?"

"Shug… I'll tell you where I lost my dignity," Tilly said, instantly appearing sober. "It was at church. On the third pew from the front or it may have been the fourth, fifth or sixth. It doesn't matter much now, does it?"

"Come up to the house and visit," Shug said, suddenly sympathetic towards Tilly. "Let's talk like old times."

"Where's Tammy Sue?" Pookie asked.

"Child welfare took her away from me and put her in foster care," Tilly answered with her head lowered. "They placed her with our fine Reverend Hurley and his milquetoast wife, Pearl. I promise you Shug… that evil man will pay for all he's done to me!"

"When you get yourself together, I'm sure they'll give Tammy Sue back," Shug reasoned.

"Maybe Pearl will, but not her conniving husband," Tilly said, releasing her grip on the door and handing June Bug's shoes to Shug. "She's a good woman. She deserves so much better than him." She then walked away before turning to say, "You and Pookie take that boy and his bad dog home."

"Tilly…." Shug stuttered.

"I'm going over there and celebrate with them," Tilly said, pointing at the two men that had taunted June bug. "Tomorrow will be a better day. You just wait and see."

Shug accepted the shoes and drove away. Tilly stood in the street for a few moments before proceeding over to where the two men stood. Like two hungry jackals, the two men surrounded Tilly. They striped her bones clean of what little dignity and respect she had left.

Shug glanced at June Bug, who had fallen asleep, and Brownie through her rear view mirror. Shug smiled at her childlike son, pondering what the future held for him. She wondered, "What am I going to do with that son of mine? What would become of him if I died before him? Would he have been better off if he weren't born?" Shug loved June Bug, but if she had to do it all over again, she would have aborted him.

Pookie was also wondering the answers to many things. "How does Johnny feel now that we've been intimate? Will I marry him someday and give birth to his children? Will our children be born retarded like June Bug?"

"Mama," Pookie said, nervously.

"What?"

"Nothing."

"Yes, it is. Go ahead and ask me."

"What's June Bug's problem?"

"What problem are you talking about?"

"I forgot."

"You didn't forget. You want to know if you got married and have children, would they be like June Bug."

"Will they?"

"Your children will be born healthy, intelligent, and beautiful. Are you thinking about having children?"

"Maybe one day… in the far future."

"Hopefully not with Johnny."

"Why?"

"Johnny is not the man for you."

"Why not?"

"You weren't at Tilly's today, either. You were with Johnny, weren't you?"

"We were just riding around in Mr. Bill's truck."

"Did you go to his house?"

"No!"

"If you say so, Pookie McAdoo! Eventually… what's done in the dark always comes to light."

Pookie wanted to ask Shug what her statement meant, but as they drove up to their house, Johnny was waiting in Mr. Bill's truck. Her heart began to race in fear that Shug would recognize something different in their body language, divulging their secret.

"Good afternoon, Miss Shug," Johnny said. "Are you glad to have Brownie back?"

"June Bug certainly is."

"Glad I could help. I just came by to tell y'all that Mr. Bill's old truck is mine now."

"He sold it to you?" Shug asked.

"No, ma'am. He gave it to me."

"That was kind of Mr. Bill," Shug said.

"Do you want me to help you get June Bug in the house?" Johnny asked.

"I would appreciate it if you took him to his room,

dressed him in some clean clothes, and put him in his bed," Shug responded. "Pookie and I will be in the kitchen."

June Bug woke up as soon as he heard Johnny's voice. For Johnny, June Bug immediately exited the car without throwing a temper tantrum.

"What's this on June Bug's face?" Johnny inquired. "And where's his clothes?"

"It's a long story," Pookie responded.

Brownie pooped in the yard before following Johnny and June Bug into the house. After Johnny put a clean shirt and a pair of briefs on June Bug, he helped him get into bed. He then went to join Shug and Pookie in the kitchen.

"All of these government houses are going to be demolished soon," Shug said unexpectedly.

"Why?" Pookie asked, jolted by Shug's announcement.

"A new neighborhood of expensive houses will be built in place of ours. Those new homes won't be for us poor people."

"Where will we go?"

"I don't have an answer," Shug replied, preparing to leave the kitchen. "But right now… I have some things I need to do in my room."

Left alone in the kitchen, Johnny and Pookie decided to go and sit on the stoop. Pookie wanted to be alone because she felt blue after so much drama had transpired, but Johnny sat next to her. He tried to kiss the worried Pookie's cheek, but she pulled away. She stared at the full moon. In her mind, she verbalized the words to what she hoped would one day become her first hit song.

"The Moon and the stars shine at the end of another long hot summer's day.

Thousands and thousands of fireflies light their merry way.

On a night like this, even the sanest people become insane.

Why do we do such stupid things?"

"Can you believe that hundreds of years ago a full moon was actually called a fool's moon?" Johnny asked.

"People do tend to get a little loony on night's like this. You could be right."

"I am right!"

"Johnny… have I been your fool?"

"No! Why do you ask such a question?"

"Because we were intimate."

"I'm sorry if you feel like I violated you. It wasn't my intention."

"It doesn't matter. What's done is done. Let's talk about something else."

"What happened to June Bug, earlier?"

"He wandered through the neighborhood and got lost. When Shug and I found him, he was trying to run away from Miss Tilly."

"I'm glad he's now safely back home," Johnny said, pulling his blue cap securely down on his head.

"Child welfare took Tammy Sue from Miss Tilly and placed her with Reverend Hurley and Mrs. Pearl."

"Mrs. Pearl must be a good woman to take care of her husband's illegitimate child."

"Is Tammy Sue Reverend Hurley's child?"

"That's the talk around town."

"I don't want to become a Tilly and have to give my child to someone else to raise. I don't want my child to be like June Bug, either."

"If I'm the father, I would never abandon you or our child."

"What if our child was retarded?"

"We won't have that problem."

"Why are you so sure?"

"You and I are not related."

"What are you trying to say?"

"Let's talk about our future," Johnny said, steering away from divulging that he had heard that June Bug was the product of an incestuous relationship. "I'm going to Chicago soon. Are you coming with me?"

"I hear Shug coming. Let's talk about it tomorrow."

Shug stopped in the doorway. She stood there for the longest time, not saying a word. When Pookie saw the deep worry lines across her mother's forehead, she decided then and there that she would not desert her family when they needed her the most. She would not be catching any train with Johnny. Instead she would stay and care for the mother and brother that had always loved her unconditionally.

While in bed, listening to the moans of the northern-bound train, Pookie would not be planning her future with Johnny as normal. She would be plotting how to secretly talk to the one person who could tell her everything she needed and wanted to know. And that person was a legally blind man named Toby.

"Bloodsuckers," Shug said, swatting at a mosquito. "I can't think of one thing a mosquito is good for!"

"Me either," Johnny added.

"A penny for your thoughts," Shug asked, looking at the distracted Pookie.

"Pookie… your mother is talking to you," Johnny said, tapping her on the shoulder.

"Sorry," Pookie said. "What did you say?"

"What's on your mind?" Shug asked.

"Nothing," Pookie responded. "I'm just a little tired and ready to go to bed."

"Me, too," Shug agreed.

"Well… I guess that's my cue to say good night," Johnny said. "I'll stop by tomorrow if that's alright with you, Miss Shug?"

"We'll be here, getting our things packed and ready to move," Shug said.

"Are we moving that soon?" Pookie asked. "Don't we have a few more weeks before we have to be out?"

"I don't want to wait too long to find another house and end up living in a shelter," Shug said, turning to go into the house. "Come on in soon, Pookie. It's getting late."

"Yes, ma'am."

"Pookie," Johnny whispered, "Don't worry about finding a place to live."

"Why not?"

"You're coming to Chicago with me. We'll leave all our worries behind."

"I can't leave Shug and June Bug in this situation! They're my family and they need me!"

"They can come with us."

"You don't mean that. And besides… Shug would never leave Alabaster."

"Who knows what tomorrow will bring?"

"Another hot day like yesterday and today," Pookie sarcastically said, standing up from the stoop. "Goodnight, Johnny."

"Goodnight. I love you, Pookie McAdoo."

Leaving Johnny outside, Pookie went inside and closed the door in his face. She regretted that she did not express that she loved him, too. She hurried back to the door, but he had already driven away.

For a few moments, everything seemed quiet, until the nightly noises of arguments and fights began. People sped through the neighborhood doing wheelies. Car stereos played loudly and horns honked for no reason. She heard the sounds of gunfire followed closely by the sirens of police, ambulances, and fire trucks.

As she slept, her cotton nightgown clung to her

body like day-old oatmeal. Finally, Pookie heard the northbound train as she dozed off to sleep.

CHAPTER 7

At five o'clock in the morning, Brownie pounced on top of Pookie and Shug's bed, licking them in the face with his sticky tongue. Having been inside overnight, he needed to go outside to defecate. However, Shug shielded her face from his licks and went back to sleep.

Pookie got out of bed and went to the front door to let him out. As soon as she opened the door, Brownie immediately ran outside. After pooping, he began to run up and down the sidewalk, barking at the drunkards who were stumbling home and the homeless who were going everywhere yet nowhere.

Speaking to Toby was all that Pookie could think about. Since Shug and June Bug were still asleep, she decided to use this time as an opportunity to visit him. She surmised that walking would take too long, giving Shug a chance to awaken and find her gone. Driving Shug's Chevrolet would be the quickest way. Although she did not have a driver's license, Pookie was willing to gamble this one time. She left Brownie outside and returned to her room to get dressed.

Pookie looked at Shug to make sure that she was

still asleep. Her eyes were rapidly twitching. This was a sign that she was having her recurring nightmare. Any other time Pookie would have awaken her, but not this morning. She could not risk her plans being spoiled.

Pookie retrieved the clothes that she had been wearing the previous day and took them into the living room. After getting dressed, she checked to make sure that June Bug was also still asleep.

As she prepared to quietly EXIT the house, she heard Shug twisting and turning in an attempt to escape from someone or something in her bad dream. Feeling guilty at allowing Shug to remain in discomfort, she decided to abandon her plans of visiting Toby and awaken her. When she reached to shake her shoulder, Shug began to talk in her sleep. Pookie listened attentively.

Shug was begging a person named Robert to leave her alone in between calling out the word "daddy." Although Pookie wanted to hear more, she began to loudly call Shug's name. With sweat pouring down her face, Shug sat up in the bed. Her fists were clinched and her eyes were wide open.

"You were having a bad dream."

"What time is it?"

"It's around seven-thirty in the morning."

"Why are you dressed so early?"

"Because when I let Brownie out to use the bathroom, he didn't come back. I was about to go and find him."

"Hurry up and find him before he gets hit by a car."

"Who's Robert?"

"I don't know. Why are you asking?"

"You said his name in your sleep."

Without answering, Shug jumped out of bed and put on the first thing that she saw. She was going to help Pookie search for Brownie. However, when they opened the front door, Johnny and Brownie were waiting on the stoop.

"Good morning," Pookie said, surprised.

"Good morning," Johnny replied.

"Johnny… why are you at my house so early?" Shug asked.

"I was on my way to the Roberson's house to help them pack for Florida and I saw Brownie running down the street. I pulled over and he jumped into the truck."

"We were just about to go and search for him," Pookie said.

"While I'm here… Mr. Bill gave me this envelope to give to you," Johnny said, handing it to Pookie.

"What's in it?" Pookie asked.

"I don't know," Johnny responded.

"Open it and see," Shug added.

"It's a hundred dollars," Pookie excitedly said, counting the twenty-dollar bills. "I only worked for thirty minutes. Certainly not long enough to earn this much money."

"Keep it for a rainy day," Shug said, turning to go into the house. She then paused in the doorway and said, "You got home mighty late to have done only thirty minutes of work. What's done in the dark always comes to the light."

"I think Shug just caught us in a lie," Johnny said, whispering.

"I think so, too."

"Yeah…."

"I booked my train ticket to Chicago. I'll be leaving in a few days."

"In a few days?"

"A scouter, who's a friend of Toby's, came in Bettie's last night. He stayed to hear me sing and play the guitar. He said that he would be my agent if I dropped everything and made my way to Chicago. Baby… I'm headed to the big time!"

"Is Toby going with you?"

"No, but you are."

"I can't right now. Shug and June Bug need me. In a few weeks, we won't even have a roof over our heads. I can't go anywhere until I know for sure that they'll be okay without me."

"How can you help them? You don't even have a job!"

"I'll just have to find one."

"Come to the club tonight and let them hear you

sing. Who knows? You may get lucky like I did."

"What would I sing?"

"What songs do you know?"

"They're mostly gospel songs."

"I know you know more than just church songs. Don't you?"

"Maybe one or two."

"Then sing one of them!"

"But, I'm a Christian."

"So," Johnny replied, chuckling. "Christians shouldn't be having sex before they're married, either! I don't want to insult you, Pookie, but we weren't having Bible study in Toby's bathroom! Now… are you coming to Bettie's tonight or not?"

"How will I get there without Shug finding out?"

"We'll think of something."

Shug then reappeared at the door. She walked down the steps, stood in the yard, and looked into the far distance. She was dressed in a new navy blue dress with matching heels. Her cleavage rose above the low cut neckline of the polyester dress. Her make-up was tastefully applied and her flawless skin amplified her natural beauty.

"You look nice," Pookie said, feeling unattractive and insecure.

"She looks fantastic," Johnny added.

"Thanks," Shug said, blushing.

"Where are you going all dressed up?" Pookie asked.

"I have a few errands to run. Fix your brother some oatmeal when he wakes up."

"Yes, ma'am."

"Johnny...." Shug said, hinting that it was time for him to leave.

"I know. It's time for me to go."

After they left, Pookie went to check on June Bug. He was under his covers and sound asleep. Brownie was on top of his bed. As Pookie stared at the drool running down the side of his open mouth, she began to wonder what life would be like if he were normal. "What if I had a normal older brother? He would be able to get a job and help Shug pay some bills. Maybe, he would drive an expensive sports car. As his little sister, I would probably beg to go with him and his girlfriend to the movies. Who knows? He may even marry and have a beautiful family of his own."

But as Pookie considered what could have been, she could not ignore the reality of the situation. June Bug was a fully-grown man with the mind of a child. He would never have a chance to experience those things. He would always be helpless, depending on someone else for his care and survival. Nevertheless, that truth did not make Pookie resent June Bug. It made her want to love and protect him even more.

Pookie then heard a knock on the door. She was hoping that Johnny had disobeyed Shug and had returned. Instead, upon opening the door, she saw a smelly and unshaven Mr. Jesse Chappelle standing on the porch. There was a time that Pookie used to get excited when he would visit and bring freshly baked brownies. But now, she barely recognized the man who had nicknamed her brother, June Bug.

"Is Shug home?"

"No, sir. She'll be back soon."

"Does she know that they're tearing down all of the houses in our neighborhood?"

"Yes, sir. She's out looking for us a place to live right now."

"How's June Bug?"

"He's okay."

"I miss seeing him. Tell Shug that I stopped by."

"Mr. Jesse… when are you moving? Where will you go?"

"I don't know. I guess time will tell."

Shortly after Mr. Jesse left, Pookie regretted that she did not ask him to watch June Bug. She reasoned that it would have given her the opportunity to go and speak to Toby. She could run the short distance to his house and make it back before Shug came home.

Pookie decided since Mr. Jesse had come to visit that she would go next door and see if he would mind babysitting for an hour. After all, he did express that he missed June Bug. Before going over to ask him, Pookie checked on June Bug. He was still asleep with Brownie lying at the foot of the bed.

Pookie then made her way through Mr. Jesse's overgrown hedges before squeezing through an opening in his rotten gate. She was shocked to see the once neat yard so badly deteriorated.

His yard was overpopulated with weeds. The flowerbeds—where beautiful roses, daffodils, and giant sunflowers used to grow—were filled with empty soda cans and broken bottles. A lawn mower, draped with spider webs, as well as the head and footboard to a bed languished in a corner of the porch. A large rusty freezer, bound with a thick chain and steel lock, was near the front door. Pookie tried her best to avoid stepping on stains that resembled blood, dripping from the bottom of it.

She knocked on the torn screen and weatherworn door, but got no answer. She then knocked harder, causing the door to slowly open on its own. Standing in the doorway, Pookie called out to Mr. Jesse. Hearing no response, she apprehensively went inside the house that she and Shug once envied for its modern furnishings and immaculate cleanliness. With Mrs. Ruby long gone, the house now reeked of pungent odors due to the infestation of rats and roaches as well as weeks-old trash.

A broken television and a pile of dirty clothes were lying on the living room floor. Pookie stepped over the trash and looked in Mr. Jesse's bedroom. There was so much clutter that she could hardly see the four posts of his bed. She again called out to him and still did not get an answer. Although she knew that she was invading his privacy, something compelled her to continue through the ghostly house.

The kitchen table, with only two legs, was tilted on its side. Three rats, nonchalant to Pookie's presence, ate molded food off of the counter. Filthy dishes filled the sink while water bugs marched across the walls.

Pookie kept her eyes on the rats while she opened the refrigerator to see if, by any chance, Mrs. Ruby's corpse was inside. The stench was so horrific that she quickly closed the door before fully checking what it contained.

At that moment, Pookie changed her mind about asking Mr. Jesse to babysit her brother. She surmised that June Bug would be safer at home alone with Brownie than in such filth.

As she prepared to leave, Pookie heard the back door opening. It was Mr. Jesse and one of the homosexual tramps that lived by the railroad tracks. Pookie quietly exited through the front door and went back to her yard without being seen.

She sat on her stoop to catch her breath. She was

thankful that Mr. Jesse had not caught her snooping around his house. But with no freshly baked brownies to share, she wondered why the sissy tramp was there. Nevertheless, more pressing matters were on her mind such as visiting Toby.

Without going back into the house, Pookie took off running down the busy highway toward his house. She silently prayed that June Bug would still be asleep by the time she returned.

As she got nearer to Toby's house, Pookie saw Mount Holy in the distance. Reverend Hurley's station wagon was outside. To her surprise, Shug's Chevrolet was parked next to his car.

Although Pookie was on her own secret mission, she was curious to know why Shug and Reverend Hurley were together. As far as she knew, they were still at odds with one another.

Pookie then detoured and ran across the churchyard. She walked up the brick steps and tried to open the door, but it was locked. Pookie went around to the door by the pastoral study. Fortunately, it was unlocked. She went inside and tiptoed toward the office next to the pulpit. As Pookie listened, she heard Shug and Reverend Hurley having a heated discussion.

"I'm not a fool like Ruby or Tilly or those other women you mess with!" Shug exclaimed. "Since it's just us two here, why don't you tell the truth and shame the devil! You were the one who fathered Ruby's unborn baby… weren't you?"

"I could've been. All Ruby had to do was let Jesse believe he was the father and everything would've been fine. But no… she had to let her emotions get in the way of common sense and tell him about our affair! Can you believe that wimp of a man even threatened to kill me over his unfaithful wife!"

"He wasn't too wimpy. I'm sure you've heard the rumor that he killed Ruby and claimed she left to cover his tracks."

"I don't know if that's true or not. That's in the past and Ruby's been gone for years now. Besides… I have another problem to worry about. Ever since Tammie Sue was placed with us, Tilly and Pearl have begun to communicate and I don't like it! I had the stupid bitch arrested for threatening to kill me and saying she'd burn this church down!"

"Is she still in jail?"

"She should be… unless my naïve wife has bailed her out."

"You son-of-a-bitch! How can you call yourself a man of God? I ought to let the entire congregation know what kind of devil you are!"

"Oh… aren't we high and mighty today with your cheap outfit on, looking like an old jezebel! I guess you figured you'd get some type of response out of me since you put your sagging breasts on full display! Sorry to disappoint you, Shug! Don't forget… you have some skeletons in your closet as well."

"Give me the damn money I need so I can get the hell out of here! For the good of every man, woman, and child—I should kill you myself!"

"Here, Judas!" Reverend Hurley shouted, as Pookie heard the sound of coins scattering across the floor. "Take your thirty pieces of silver and get the hell out of here… you inbred bitch!"

"Judas," Shug replied in a devious grin. "When it comes to you… Reverend… I'm more like Ehud and you're Eglon, king of Moab!"

Shug and Reverend Hurley continued to rant and rave at each other. Pookie wanted to intervene, but Shug would have been outraged that if she discovered that she was spying on her and equally angered that she had left June Bug alone. Fearful that Shug would more than likely be on her way back home soon, Pookie determined it was best to again abandon her plans of visiting Toby and quickly run back home.

Shug and Reverend Hurley's argument preoccupied Pookie's thoughts so much so that she did not realize that she was getting dangerously close to the incoming traffic. If one driver had not veered to the left, he would have struck her with his car. Pulling over to the side of the road, the driver rolled down his window and screamed obscenities at Pookie. He then asked her if she was trying to commit suicide.

As the irate man chastised Pookie, Mrs. Pearl suddenly drove by in Tyrone's car. Tilly was in the passenger seat. They were heading in the direction of Mount Holy. Luckily the man's car blocked their view, preventing them from seeing her. Pookie wondered if things could get any worse.

When Pookie finally got home, a crowd of people was standing on the sidewalk near her house. To her horror, Mr. Jesse's house was engulfed in flames. Black smoke polluted the air, causing Pookie and many in the crowd to cough. She did not think it was possible for her heart to beat any faster, but it did. Worried at the possibility that June Bug might have awakened and wandered into the fire, Pookie's legs began to tremble.

She opened her front door so quickly that it nearly hit Brownie, who was waiting at the door, wagging his tail. As he dashed outside, Pookie went directly to June Bug's room. She was about to hyperventilate when she heard noises coming from the kitchen. She dashed into the kitchen while praying that God forgive her for her sins.

Pookie then found June Bug with a white powdery substance all over his face and clothes. She assumed that he had gotten into the bag of flour. He looked like Casper the friendly ghost as he stood, staring at his younger sister. She was elated to find her brother safe. Attempting to conceal from Shug that she had left him alone, Pookie quickly swept up the mess before returning outside. Her focus was now on checking on her neighbor, Mr. Jesse, and making sure the fire was not spreading in the direction of their small, wood-framed house.

"What happened?" Pookie asked an onlooker, as the fire department was just arriving.

"They think Mr. Jesse is trapped inside," the man answered. "He's probably burnt to a crisp by now!"

"How did this happen?" Pookie asked. "I mean… I just…."

"I don't know," a woman interrupted. "When I was

on my way to the liquor store, I heard a loud explosion. The house just burst into flames. These houses are so raggedy, it might have been a gas leak."

The fire marshals then started to shoo people away. Pookie reluctantly went back home, saddened at the thought that Mr. Jesse may have met his demise in the fire. Though mournful, she was relieved that she had not asked him to babysit June Bug.

When she returned to her house, Johnny was parking in her driveway. He again had Brownie with him. Even before he got out of the truck, Pookie noticed that something was different about him. She realized that he was not wearing his blue Bill's Hardware cap.

"I can't believe Mr. Jesse's house burnt down," Johnny said, quickly getting out of the truck. "I came over as soon as I heard."

"Someone said he might've died in the fire!"

"Are you sure?"

"That's what I heard."

"That's weird because I could've sworn that I saw him when I was out by the train station, delivering some cable."

“Well… did you talk to him?”

“No, I didn’t.”

“Hmmm….”

“But, I’m sure it was him… unless… I was mistaken.”

“Let’s hope you’re right and he wasn’t in that house!”

“Why are you staring at me?”

“You look different without that cap stuck on top of your head.”

“I guess I left it at home,” Johnny said, feeling the top of his head.

“So what did you and Miss Shug decide to do?”

“We don’t know where we’re moving to.”

“Well… y’all better think of something soon. It’s just a matter of time before those white folks give the word and this neighborhood disappears like it never existed.”

"You're probably right."

"I know I'm right," Johnny said, continuing to touch his head. "Where's June Bug?"

"He's in the house."

"Alone? We better go and check on him."

Pookie and Johnny went into the house with Brownie following closely behind. They found June Bug lying on his back. He was rubbing his stomach and moaning. His face looked pale and extremely gaunt. It was obvious that he was very sick.

"What could've made him so sick?" Johnny inquired.

"I don't know," Pookie replied, stressed and nervous.

"He looks horrible."

"Maybe he's just hungry. It's been a long time since he last ate."

"What have you been doing all morning?"

"June Bug and I slept late."

"A house burns down next door and you slept through it?"

"I guess I was tired."

"Cook June Bug some oatmeal while I take him to the bathroom."

Pookie stared into the refrigerator while trying to make sense of everything that had happened. Her mind was cluttered with so many questions that mystified her. She wondered, "What caused Mr. Jesse's house to burn down? Was he trapped inside or had Johnny really seen him near the train station? What happened to the sissy tramp that was at his house? Did he set the fire or did he perish in it as well? Why were Shug and Reverend Hurley saying such cruel things to one another?"

She was still staring aimlessly into the refrigerator when Johnny brought June Bug into the kitchen and sat him down at the table.

"Are you waiting for the oatmeal to jump into your hands?" Johnny teased.

"No," Pookie responded, startled. "I just got a lot on my mind."

Leaving the refrigerator door open, Pookie filled a

small pot with water. She then searched for a box of matches to light the burner. Upon observing Pookie rummaging through drawers, Johnny took a lighter from his pocket and lit it for her.

Pookie set the pot on the burner and poured oatmeal into it. She then sat next to June Bug, who occasionally rested his head on her shoulder. After a few minutes, Johnny brought the pot of oatmeal and a spoon over to the table. He attempted to feed June Bug, but he would not eat.

"I signed a contract today with that guy I was telling you about. He's officially my agent now."

"I'm happy for you."

"You don't sound like it."

"I really am Johnny. It's just I…."

"Aren't you coming with me?"

"I can't leave Shug and June Bug! It wouldn't be fair."

"Toby said they could move in with him."

"That's kind of him, but…."

"You don't understand, Pookie! I got to get out of this town!"

"I wish I could leave, too!"

"Then come with me."

"Shug and June Bug…."

"You have two days to make up your mind. In two days from today, I'll be leaving Alabaster on one of those trains we always hear!"

Their conversation was interrupted by the arrival of Shug. When Brownie heard her come into the kitchen, he came from under June Bug's bed and followed her. He lay under June Bug's chair and began to wag his tail to the rhythm of the dripping faucet in the kitchen sink.

Shug did not exhibit any anger when she saw Johnny alone in the house with Pookie. Instead, she and Johnny appeared unusually glad to see each other. She kissed June Bug on his forehead, but his reaction was abnormal. He would normally plaster his sticky kisses all over Shug's face. However, on this day, he only incoherently stared.

"Did you hear about Mr. Jesse?" Johnny asked.

"Yes, I did," Shug said as she again kissed June Bug. "Tilly told me about it right before I came in."

"That's so sad," Pookie added.

"Jesse can…." Shug said before turning her attention to her son. "What's wrong with June Bug?"

"I don't think he feels good," Pookie responded.

"Come on, Son," Shug said, taking June Bug by the hand and guiding him to his feet. "A warm bath will make you feel better."

"Miss Shug," Johnny said, "Toby told me to tell you that you're welcome to stay with him until y'all find a place."

"We would hate to put Toby in a bind, but right now… we don't have much of a choice," Shug replied.

"I agree," Pookie said.

"You have two more days to make up your mind if you're leaving with me," Johnny whispered in Pookie's ear as he prepared to leave. "I'll see you later Miss Shug."

"Thanks for everything, Johnny," Shug responded,

as Pookie contemplated what he had whispered. "Before you go… would you mind running Pookie to get June Bug some soup?"

"It'll be my pleasure," Johnny responded.

Pookie assumed Shug had taken a strange liking to Johnny to allow her to leave the house with him. Either that or she was simply too exhausted to drive the short distance to the corner store herself. Pookie, however, saw this as the chance she had been waiting for.

"Johnny… take me to see Toby."

"Why?"

"I just want to talk to him."

"Talk to him about what?"

"I want to speak to him about us moving in with him." Seeing that Johnny was taking a different route, Pookie inquired about the reason. "Why are we going this way?"

"The traffic isn't as heavy this way."

"I wanted you to drive by Mount Holy!"

"Why?"

"That way reminds me of our first outing together."

The compliment stroked Johnny's male ego, accomplishing what Pookie wanted. He smiled, turned the truck around, and headed in the direction of Mount Holy. However, the closer they got to the church, the more agitated Johnny seemed to become.

As they approached, Pookie could see flashing lights from police cars. The church was being cordoned off with yellow police tape. A crowd was forming near the church's entrance. Parishioners, as well as curious bystanders, were parking their vehicles at a distance and walking closer to get a better view. Other drivers were turning around to avoid the potential traffic jam.

"Johnny... what's happening at my church?"

"I don't know."

"Let's pull over and see!"

"I'm going to be late for work if I do. The band will be expecting me soon."

"I'll just walk to Toby's house from here."

"I'm not going to let you walk. Miss Shug wants me to drive you back!"

"Trust me! I'll be fine."

"Before you leave Uncle Toby's, call me at the club and I'll sneak away to take you home."

After getting out of the truck, Pookie eventually made her way into the middle of the gathering of people. She recognized one of the onlookers as Sister Christine Johnson.

"What happened?" Pookie asked.

"Pearl and Tilly found Reverend Hurley," Sister Johnson answered, unable to contain her tears.

"Found him where?" Pookie asked, confused.

"Sitting on one of the pews… dead from a stab wound to his stomach."

A stunned Pookie then saw Mrs. Pearl, Alspice, and Tilly walking from behind the church. Alspice hysterically sobbed as the emergency medical technicians loaded Reverend Hurley's deceased body, enclosed in a black body bag, into the waiting ambulance. Pookie, along with the inquisitive crowd, watched as Mrs. Pearl sped away to follow them.

As Pookie journeyed on to Toby's house, her heart ached for Alspice.

Pookie could hear Toby moving around inside of the house when she knocked on the door. After she knocked several more times, he finally answered.

"Who is it?"

"It's me… Pookie."

"Johnny isn't home right now."

"I didn't come to see Johnny. I came to see you."

"Well… to what do I owe this pleasure?"

"I need some questions answered."

"Come on in the kitchen. I was just about to make me a sandwich."

"I have bad news about my neighbor, Mr. Jesse. His house burned down today and someone told me that he was trapped inside."

"Oh my… that's horrible!"

"And Reverend Hurley…."

"Horace was in the house with Jesse?"

"No… no… someone stabbed him to death inside of Mount Holy! I saw the police and ambulance there when I was walking over here."

"Well… this is shocking news! But, I can't answer any questions about their deaths. I didn't know until you just informed me."

"That's not why I'm here. I want to know about some other things that have been eating at me."

Toby pulled a chair out from the table for Pookie to sit. She silently watched as he prepared two sandwiches, one for each of them. He took a jar of mayonnaise and a pitcher of iced tea out of the refrigerator. He set them on the table next to a loaf of bread and a platter of sliced ham, tomatoes, and lettuce. He then got two plates and two glasses from the cabinet and also set them on the table.

"Cat got your tongue?" Toby asked as he made the sandwiches and filled the glasses with tea.

"No… I was just thinking."

"Stop thinking and eat your sandwich," Toby said, handing her a plate. "I make a superb ham sandwich."

"It's delicious," Pookie responded as she took a bite. She was amazed that a legally blind man could take such good care of himself.

"Are Shug and June Bug coming to stay with me?"

"What about me?" Pookie asked, feeling left out.

"Aren't you leaving with Johnny?"

"It depends."

"Depends on what?"

"What you tell me about my mother."

"What makes you think that I know anything about your mother?"

"I heard you and Shug talking."

"Yeah… Johnny told me that y'all were hiding in his room that day. I'm sorry that you overheard our conversation."

"I'm glad that I did because… what you tell me to-day will help me decide if I go with Johnny or stay in Alabaster."

"I'm all ears then Miss McAdoo."

"Please tell me everything you know and don't hold back."

"It's not pretty."

"I can take the truth! I must know or I'll drive myself crazy trying to fill in the gaps myself."

"Okay," Toby said, taking a deep breath. "I met your mama when she was staying with her father, Lewis, and her uncle, Robert. They were living in Columbus, Georgia at the time."

"What about her mother?" Pookie asked, interrupting. "Where was she? What was her name?"

"I can't remember Shug ever talking about her mother."

"What about…."

"Pookie… I warned you that it's not a pretty story, but you're insisting on knowing so let me finish!"

"Sorry, Toby."

"The first time I saw Shug was when I drove by her house on my way to run an errand for my grandmother. She couldn't have been anymore than fifteen years old. I would always she her sitting in a swing on her porch. One day… I finally got up enough courage to stop and talk to her. I boldly walked up and spoke. I could sense that she was sad, lonely, and very troubled. I told her that my name was Thomas and that my friends call me Toby. And that's how we met."

"What kind of people were Lewis and Robert?"

"No one knew much about them. I always talked with Shug on the porch. Although they were in the house, neither ever took the time to introduce themselves."

"Did you ever take her for a ride?"

"We never left that porch or went into the house. Sometimes, I would bring my guitar and play it or sing blues songs to her. Shug loved the blues. I really fell hard for your mama. I asked her to be my girlfriend and she said she would."

"What happened?"

"Everything just started to unravel. At eighteen, I was drafted into the army. Shug and I often wrote each other. Before my nineteenth birthday, I was hit by shrapnel and lost most of my eyesight. I was devastated and didn't tell her about it. When I was discharged, I planned on coming home and telling her, but chickened out. I let Bettie persuade me to move to Europe and begin a music career. I couldn't let Shug be burdened with a helpless, nearly blind man like myself. I felt she deserved more than what I could offer her at the time. But surprisingly, the Europeans loved my music and I made tons of money. I didn't save much, but I sure was making it. Five years later, I returned home to attend the funeral of my dear grandmother. While in town, I was going to ask Shug to marry me, but it was too late."

"How so?"

"She was gone. I asked anyone and everyone I could if they knew where she went. No one could tell me, but they had no problem spreading evil gossip about her."

"What were they saying?"

"I believe you deserve to know the truth. Maybe it will help you understand your mother better."

"I believe so, too."

"Her father, Lewis, moved away and left her alone in the house with her uncle, Robert."

"And…."

"He began molesting her. Pookie… between you and me… June Bug is retarded because he is the product of incest. Robert is his daddy."

"I think I've met the slime-ball before," Pookie mumbled.

"I doubt you've ever seen June Bug's father. He was murdered behind the gas station where he used to work."

"You're probably right," Pookie responded, now more positive than ever that the man they encountered at the gas station was indeed the same person. "I'm sure I've never met him."

"Rumor has it that after your brother was born, Robert stayed around for a while and then disappeared. Shug and her disabled baby were forced to live in homeless shelters. I didn't see or hear from her again until she walked into Bettie's looking for you. I recognized her voice as soon as she began to talk. To me… it sounded just like the sweet innocent teenager I used to know."

"Do you know who my father is?"

"Honestly, Pookie… I have no idea."

"I believe you."

"I know you do."

"Toby… thanks so much for being honest. What you said will forever remain between us. My lips are sealed."

"I'm glad I could help you."

"Do you have two cans of soup that I can borrow?"

"There are some cans of chicken noodle soup in the cabinet. Help yourself."

"Thanks."

"So… now that your questions have been answered… are you going to Chicago with Johnny?"

"I'm not going to desert Shug like her father and uncle did. I'm staying right here with her and my brother."

"And she has never and will never desert you and June Bug either."

"Toby… can you get me a job at Bettie's?"

"Doing what?"

"Singing with the band."

"I see you've grown very confident in yourself."

"Maybe that was asking too much," Pookie blushed. "I'm willing to start as a waitress."

"Now, now… don't let me dampen your dreams. But… you'll have to prove yourself to Bettie, who can be a little strange sometimes."

"I hope everything works out."

"If you really want a job as a singer, I'll do what I can to help you."

"I don't know how I'll ever repay you for what you're doing for me and my family."

"I'm just happy that I can finally do something for Shug."

"Promise me that you won't say anything to Johnny about my decision. I want to tell him myself."

"Scout's honor."

"Great!"

"How are you getting home?"

"I'm walking."

"It's too late and dangerous for you to walk! Use my phone and call Johnny. He'll come and drive you home."

"Johnny will be grilling me with questions that I don't feel like answering right now. I promise you… I'll be fine."

Toby escorted Pookie to the door and she began her trek home. From a distance, she could see him standing in his doorway. She waved to him and he immediately waved back.

"Silly me… waving to a blind man," Pookie said to herself. But then she wondered, "How could Toby have waved back if he's blind?"

The evening was turning dusky. Pookie felt a chill go through her bones. As she walked past Mount Holy, she sensed Reverend Hurley's presence. Pookie began to run, holding on tightly to the bag of soup. She did not stop until she was safely back inside her house.

Shug was in the living room, sitting on the faded floral sofa as she waited for her to return. Observing the helpless look on her mother's face made Pookie determined to never let Shug discover what Toby had disclosed about her childhood.

In an attempt to temporarily escape from her own uncertainties, worries, doubts, and fears—Pookie sat next to Shug and wrote her name in the layers of dust on the coffee table.

"You were gone a long time," Shug said with dark bags under her eyes. "I was beginning to worry."

"How's June Bug?"

"He seems to be doing better. I'll keep an eye on him throughout the night."

"That's good to hear."

"Do you have soup in that bag?"

"Yes, ma'am. I got him some cans of chicken noodle soup."

"Good thing you came on home. It's going to be a stormy night."

"Maybe the rain will wash away some of the agony

we've experienced today."

"Agony like what?"

"Like Mr. Jesse and…." Pookie said, before deciding not to mention Reverend Hurley's death."

"And…."

"And nothing. I'm just tired."

"Let's go to bed so we can wake up early to a new day… a new beginning."

"Can I lay here, on the sofa, for a while?"

"Okay, but don't stay up too long."

Pookie laid on the sofa, trying to rest her weary and discontented soul. However, the constant noises coming from the street and the information she learned from Toby, coupled with the deaths of Mr. Jesse and Reverend Hurley, would not allow her.

With her mind boggled with thoughts, Pookie was reminded of what Shug had said about a new day bringing a new beginning. She pondered, "What good is another day when all of yesterday's baggage comes with it? Shug will begin her tomorrow like all of the others. She'll rise early and get dressed.

With an empty trash bag, she'll go outside and fill it with all of the discarded cans of beer, broken whiskey bottles, and used condoms thrown in our yard. What could possibly happen worse than anything we've already experienced?"

Pookie then heard the northern bound train, humming its familiar tune. On this particular night, the sound saddened her like no other.

Before finally dozing off to sleep, she whispered, "Will I ever ride that train?"

Pookie did not know the answer to that question, but one thing was certain. She would not be riding it with Johnny. As it stood, he would be catching it alone, for Pookie had unequivocally made up her mind that she would remain in Alabaster alongside her beloved mother and brother.

CHAPTER 8

The misty rain, blowing through the slightly open window, awakened Pookie. Her face and the sofa were damp. She walked to the window and looked outside. The street was deserted like a ghost town. Not a single person was in view.

"What are you looking at?" Shug asked.

"Nothing," Pookie answered, surprised. "I didn't know you were up."

"We got another leak in the kitchen."

"What's that noise coming from the walls?"

"It's those damn rodents! If I could find my bag of rat poison, I'd kill those suckers!"

"Don't worry about the rats. We'll be moving to Toby's house soon."

"You're not going with Johnny?"

"How did you know I was thinking about leaving with him?"

"I know a lot more than you think I do! Have you told him you're not going?"

"Not yet," Pookie responded, wondering what other of her secrets Shug knew.

"When are you going to tell him?"

"I'm going to tell him today."

"If you want to leave with Johnny… June Bug and I will be fine."

"I've decided to stay and I won't be changing my mind."

"I'm glad you did. It's early… why don't you get a little more sleep?"

"I'm not tired now. Besides… if I get a job singing nights at Bettie's, my days of getting up early will be over. I'll need all the sleep I can get. I might as well enjoy the morning breezes while I can."

"Singing at Bettie's," Shug said, startled by the revelation.

"Johnny said he'd tell Toby to put in a good word for me with Bettie."

"That Bettie is one strange person. I guess if anyone can help you get hired, it's Toby."

"Let's keep our fingers crossed!"

"If you get the job, can June Bug and I come and hear you sing?"

"You would come to hear me sing at Bettie's?"

"Of course I would. You just get the job and we'll cross that bridge when we get there."

"Did you hear that?" Pookie asked, making sure she was not hearing things.

"It sounds like moaning," Shug replied, listening more attentively. "It must be June Bug!"

Shug and Pookie immediately hurried into June Bug's room. They found him on top of his bed, balled into a fetal position. He was perspiring heavily, causing his shirt and briefs to become soaked. He cried out in pain when Shug gently touched him.

"What's the matter with him?" Pookie asked. "I thought he was improving?"

"I don't know, but it seems serious! I better get him to the emergency room!"

"Is there anything I can do?"

"Get the keys off of my dresser and start the car while I'm getting dressed!"

Shug had forgotten to roll up the windows. The car seats were moist due to the rain. Pookie sat on the wet seat and started the engine. Shug then helped June Bug out to the car. He was still dressed in his underclothes, and a blanket was wrapped around him.

"I want you to drive," Shug requested of Pookie.

"Are you sure?"

"I need to sit in the back with June Bug!"

June Bug's constant cries, plus her limited driving experience, unnerved Pookie. Unsympathetic drivers honked their horns or gave her the finger when she drove too slowly or veered slightly out of her lane.

Once they finally arrived at the hospital, Pookie stopped in front of the emergency room entrance to let Shug and June Bug out of the car. She then went to park near the door. However, a security guard demanded that she park somewhere else. After finding another parking space, she ran into the waiting room.

It was filled with sick and injured people waiting to see a doctor. To pass the time, most watched a television that was bolted to the wall.

A friendly hospital employee, with long auburn hair, came into the room. Her red and white striped apron was crisply ironed and her green eyes sparkled. She looked around in pity at everyone before calling Pookie's name.

"Yes, ma'am. I'm Pookie McAdoo."

"Your mother is waiting for you. She's in the lounge on the eighth floor."

After exiting the elevator, Pookie found Shug sitting next to a window. In between looking out at the parking lot, she played a game of patty cake with her hands and knees in an attempt to mask her nervousness.

"Is June Bug Okay?" Pookie asked, somewhat hysterical.

"I don't know. They're still trying to find out what's wrong with him."

"Why aren't you with him?"

"The doctor said that it was best for me to wait out

here."

"I hope it's nothing too serious."

Shug and Pookie waited for an update on June Bug's condition. The minutes slowly passed before a doctor finally came to speak to them.

"Shug McAdoo… I'm Dr. John Moss."

"Nice to meet you doctor. How's my son?"

"Well at the moment… I've been unable to exactly pinpoint the cause of his illness. Is your son on any medications or special diets?"

"No. He mostly eats the same foods everyday."

"Have you noticed any changes in his appetite?"

"Not particularly."

"Is it possible that he could have digested something poisonous?"

"No. Either myself or his sister keeps a good eye on him."

"Because people with his condition have a higher

probability of dying very young, we need to take special care with his treatment plan. Not only does he have one of the most profound cases of mental retardation that my staff has ever seen, but he also has an enlarged heart. His sudden bout of sickness may be the result of natural causes related to his already deteriorating health."

"Is there anything that can be done? Please Dr. Moss… save my sweet son!"

"I'm sorry to tell you that June Bug has been placed in a medically-induced coma."

"Oh God!"

"We will continue doing everything we can to save him. If you follow me… you can visit him for a while."

Dr. Moss then escorted Shug and Pookie into June Bug's room. A machine that was monitoring his heart stood near his bed. He had tubes coming from his arms, nose, and throat. Using the back of her hand, Shug gently stroked June Bug's face.

Dr. Moss tried to persuade Shug to go home and get some rest until further notice. He promised to summon her back as soon as his condition changed. Shug, however, insisted on staying by June Bug's bedside.

Shug then requested that Pookie return home to get some of June Bug's belongings and to let Brownie out to use the bathroom. Out of fear that she could not drive without assistance, Shug told Pookie to call Johnny so he could give her a ride home.

As Pookie waited for Johnny, she leaned against Shug's Chevrolet. She was relieved when his truck finally arrived and he waved for her to get in.

"Is there any news on June Bug's condition?"

"No more than what I told you over the telephone," Pookie responded, noticing three large suitcases on the back of his truck. "Are you already packed to leave?"

"This is a bad time to say this, but I'm leaving today," Johnny said, avoiding eye contact. "Opportunity has knocked and if I don't let it in, it may never knock again."

"I understand," Pookie said in a monotone voice. "I suppose you have to do what you have to do."

"Are you coming with me?"

"I told you over the telephone that June Bug could

die! I can't leave Shug right now! I'll have to meet you there later once all of this mess is over."

"I promise to write you, Pookie McAdoo. Whenever you're ready to come, you'll know where I am."

"After I get some things from the house, will you drive me back to the hospital?"

"I have a surprise for you. After we leave your house, I want you to go with me to the train station. Once I get my suitcases off the back, my truck is yours."

"That's very kind of you, Johnny," Pookie said, fighting back tears. "I don't know what to say."

"Just say 'thanks.'"

Overwhelmed by June Bug's sudden illness and the news that today would be Johnny's last day in Alabaster—Pookie began to sob uncontrollably. People driving by or waiting at the traffic light began to notice. Johnny handed her his handkerchief so she could wipe away her tears. She had barely stopped crying when they arrived at her house.

When she opened the front door, Brownie quickly ran outside. Pookie called his name, but he continued to run down the street.

Pookie searched June Bug's closet and shabby dresser drawers for suitable pieces of clothing to take to the hospital. Johnny walked up behind her as she searched. He held her close with the same intensity as he had done when they were intimate. But today, they were not in Toby's neat bathroom. They were in her unkempt home from which she and her family would soon be evicted.

"It'll be a long time before we see each other again," Johnny said, softly kissing Pookie. I want to experience what we did in Toby's bathroom once more before I go."

"I just can't right now," Pookie responded, placing her hand against his chest in an attempt to ward off his advances. "Please get me a grocery bag from the kitchen so I can pack these clothes."

Johnny went to retrieve a bag as Pookie neatly folded June Bug's dingy white t-shirts, holey boxer shorts, and mismatched socks. She then got his toothbrush off of his bedside table. As Pookie placed the items into the small bag, she vowed that one day she would be rich enough that her family would never again have to wear thrift store clothes or use plastic bags as luggage.

Unbeknownst to Johnny, Pookie was staring into his eyes as he waited patiently by the door. She could tell that he was engulfed with planning out the successful musical career that awaited him. Pookie wished that she were instead packing her belongings to leave with him on his journey to fame. Their paths, which had seemed so in tune before, had now begun to diverge. Only the future knew what detours their lives would take or what roadblocks lay ahead. Would their paths ever cross again?

Pookie and Johnny could not find Brownie when they were ready to leave. They continuously called for him, but he did not return. Pookie left enough water and food on the porch to sustain him until she could return. Together, Pookie and Johnny then began what would be their last ride through her vanishing neighborhood.

From the rear view mirror, Pookie saw Tilly taking bags of trash and broken furniture out to the curb. When Tilly recognized that it was Johnny and Pookie, she began to wave her hands for them to stop. Pookie told Johnny to turn around so she could see what Tilly, who was discarding a pee-stained mattress, wanted.

Pookie was surprised to see Tilly dressed in clean clothes and completely sober.

"Where's Shug?" Tilly inquired, dumping the last bag of trash on top of the mattress. "I've got something to tell her."

"She's at the hospital."

"Is Shug sick?"

"No, ma'am. It's June Bug."

"What's wrong with him?"

"The doctors don't know, but he's in a coma."

"What hospital is he at?"

"He's at City Hospital on Chestnut Street in room eight thirty one."

"This moving can wait! I'm going to be with Shug and June Bug!"

"After I drop Johnny off at the train station, you can ride with me."

"Johnny… are you are going somewhere?" Tilly asked, wiping sweat from her face.

"Yes, ma'am. I'm going to Chicago."

"When are you coming back?"

"I don't plan on ever coming back."

"What about Pookie?"

"She'll join me later."

"I'm glad… because she loves you."

"If you don't mind Miss Tilly… what did you want to tell my mother?" Pookie asked, embarrassed by their conversation.

"I want to tell Shug that I'm turning my life around for the better," Tilly proudly responded. "I've stopped drinking and want us to be good friends just like before. Pearl has already forgiven me for…. Well, that's between Pearl and me. She even invited me to live at her house. I'll have a place to stay and be with my daughter, Tammy Sue!"

"I'm so happy for you Miss Tilly!" Pookie said.

"Me too," Johnny agreed, looking down at his watch. "We must get going before I miss my train."

"I'll see you later Miss Tilly," Pookie said as they drove away.

Passengers were already boarding the train when Pookie and Johnny arrived at the station. He told

Pookie to wait in the truck until he went inside to check his luggage and confirm his ticket.

A few minutes later, Johnny returned. He handed Pookie the keys to his truck before gently pecking her on the lips.

"I must go now," Johnny said, in an anxious voice. "My train is about to leave."

"I'm going to miss you, Johnny Overtree, and I'll never forget you," Pookie said with tears streaming down her cheeks.

"You better not," Johnny replied, releasing her hand. He then walked backwards, as they stared at one another, until he reached the entrance of the station. Johnny shouted, "I'll always love you Pookie McAdoo," before disappearing inside.

There were so many things that Pookie had wanted to say to Johnny, but the words remained stuck in her throat. She would have liked to tell him how much she loved him and that she did not want him to leave. But as she drove away, the sounds of his train departing the station reminded her that it was too late. Johnny had done what he always claimed he would do, which was to leave the godforsaken town of Alabaster in search of fame. As Pookie headed towards the EXIT, she whispered, "I love you too, Johnny!"

The drive back was especially heart wrenching for Pookie. She was not yet mentally prepared to return to the hospital. She decided to visit Toby, the closest person to the man she now missed more than words could express.

When she pulled into his driveway, he was sitting in a swing on the porch. His eyes were shielded from the beaming sun by a pair of dark glasses. Pookie got out of the truck and sat next to him.

"So… you decided not to go," Toby said upon hearing her voice.

"Not now," Pookie responded with her head hanging low. "Johnny gave me his truck."

"He said that he would if you decided not to leave with him."

"Thanks for letting us move in with you."

"You're very welcome. Since you have the truck… you can move some of your belongings in today."

"I can't today. I got to go back to the hospital."

"Johnny told me that June Bug was sick. How's he

doing?"

"Not well."

"If I didn't have to work, I'd ride with up there and visit him and Shug."

"Do you need me to give you a lift to work?"

"No, thanks. Raymond is coming for me."

"Have you had a chance to talk to Bettie about giving me a job?"

"Yes… and the job is yours."

"Are you sure?"

"As sure as the day is long. When June Bug is better… come on down to the club so Bettie can meet you."

"I sure will."

"Bettie is a pussycat, so don't be intimidated."

"Thanks, Toby. My family and I will be forever grateful to you."

"You're very welcome."

"Shug must be wondering what happened to me," Pookie said, standing up from the swing. "I better get back to the hospital."

"I'll be staying at Bettie's for a few days," Toby said, handing her a spare key to his house. "You live here now. You're welcome to relax a little before you leave for the hospital."

"Thanks Toby. I think I'll do just that."

"You can rest in Johnny's room. I made sure he left it ready for you."

"We don't want to run you away from your own home?"

"You're not. I often stay overnight at Bettie's."

When Pookie went inside, she immediately went to the telephone. She dialed the hospital to speak to Shug.

"City Hospital… may I help you."

"June Bug's room please."

"We don't have a June Bug."

"I'm sorry. I meant James McAdoo. June Bug is his nickname."

"Who's speaking?"

"His sister, Annie Lee McAdoo. But, they call me Pookie."

"One moment while I connect you."

The phone to June Bug's room rang and rang as Pookie's heart pounded and pounded. She wanted to let Shug know why she had not returned. She was worried that the continuous ringing meant something was wrong. Shug finally answered the phone as soon as Pookie was preparing to jet out of the house and speed back to the hospital.

"Hello."

"It's me… Pookie."

"I've been worried about you!"

"I'm just at Toby's house. How's June Bug?"

"He's the same."

"Johnny left for Chicago today."

"I know you probably don't believe me, but I'm sorry he's gone."

"I believe you. He gave me his truck."

"You know you don't have a driver's license. What if you get stopped by the police and get a ticket? We don't have money to pay any fines."

"I'll be careful."

"Is Toby all right with us moving in with him?"

"Yes, ma'am. He gave me a spare key."

"Great."

"He said that he was looking forward to our company."

"Well… that's nice."

"Have you eaten anything?"

"Yes… Tilly took a taxi here to see June Bug and we ate in the cafeteria."

"I was supposed to go back and get her. I'm glad she made it up there."

"Tilly has stopped drinking. She told me that she's going to live with Pearl and Tammy Sue!"

"That's wonderful," Pookie responded, pretending she was not already privy to the information.

"I hope Pearl and I can rekindle our friendship, too."

"Wasn't it strange the way Reverend Hurley died?"

"Where's Toby?" Shug asked, quickly changing the subject.

"Raymond came to get him. I heard them drive away when I was waiting for you to answer the phone."

"Okay… well I'll call you back shortly."

"I'll probably be back at the hospital before then."

"It's too late for you to be driving that truck! Tilly is coming back to keep me company. Just stay there for tonight. Tomorrow morning, you can take the truck and begin moving our things."

Yes, ma'am."

"We need to get out stuff out of that house. The city wants those homes demolished sooner than what we had been expecting."

"Where am I going to put all of our junk?"

"That junk is all we have Pookie McAdoo. Ask Toby if we can store it in his garage. When we move into our own place, we'll need that junk as you call it."

"Can we buy some new furniture?"

"With a sick child and no job, how do you expect me to afford new furniture?"

"I have a job!"

"Where?"

"At Bettie's."

"Are you sure?"

"Well… almost sure."

"Tell me all about it tomorrow. I have to hang up now because the nurse is coming in to check on June Bug."

As Pookie walked into Johnny's room, she smelled the scent of his cologne. Thoughts of when they had made love in the bathroom before hiding from Shug and Toby made her giggle. She reminisced back to all the times they had shared such as fighting with

Alspice at Mount Holy, almost being run over by Reverend Hurley, and driving endlessly around in his truck. She smiled at the memories of him sitting on her stoop early in the morning or late at night, waiting for her until Shug would run him off.

But, those times were now in the past. Her smiles turned to frowns as she contemplated other pressing things in her life. She laid on top of the covers in her clothes and shoes. Grasping tightly to the pillow, her cluttered mind began to wonder. "I hope Brownie is safe. By now, he's probably waiting at the door so he can come in and sleep on June Bug's bed. I bet he could heal my brother just by making him laugh or licking him on his face.

She then thought of the neighborhood where she and her family had been living for the last several years. "Where will our evicted neighbors go to live? Will the homeless find a new place to steal a good night's sleep? Will the gangs find another community to terrorize? Where will the tramps, who hang out by the railroad, go?"

In between all of those thoughts and the sweet scent of Johnny's cologne, Pookie eventually fell asleep.

CHAPTER 9

Pookie drove the truck to her house to move her belongings. Raymond, the drummer at Mount Holy and Bettie's Blues Barn, followed her in his van to help.

Upon their arrival, Pookie did not find Brownie waiting on the stoop. However, she did discover that her front door had been kicked in and thieves had vandalized her home.

Pookie and Raymond cautiously went inside and surveyed every room. Just about everything was either stolen or destroyed. The house was completely trashed. Quilts that covered their beds were gone, dresser drawers that held their secondhand clothes were bare, and sheets used to cover their windows were removed. The leaky washing machine, scratched table, and mismatched chairs were taken. The refrigerator lay on its side, signifying the robbers' attempt to move it before deciding it was too heavy, and the little food it had held was scattered all over the kitchen floor. Only a small bag of dog food and a pile of dirty clothes in the bathtub remained.

As she prepared to leave, she glanced in June Bug's

room. Miraculously, his blue suit and white shirt were still hanging in his closet. While grabbing it from the hangers, Pookie surmised that perhaps even criminals have sympathy for a sick person.

Before Pookie and Raymond left the vandalized house, she made sure that Brownie's bowl was full of water and that he could find the last few morsels of dog food next to June Bug's old rusty wagon. Pookie retrieved a few pieces of Shug's dirty clothing from the bathtub and with no belongings to now move into storage, she took one last ride through her vanishing neighborhood. Raymond followed closely behind her.

One by one, the houses were becoming empty. Men and women were loading their belongings onto trucks as their children placed bags of garbage near the curbs. The little boys and girls stopped what they were doing and stared at the red truck as it passed. Pookie pretended not to see the sadness in their snot-stained faces.

When Pookie got back to Toby's house, she remained sitting in the truck. She was tired, hungry, and without clean clothes to wear. Upon parking behind her, Raymond got out of his van and sat in the truck next to her.

"What are you going to tell your mother about the

house being vandalized?"

"I'm going to tell her the truth. The things that I'm wearing are the only clothes I have."

"Are you coming to meet Bettie today?"

"That was my plan, but this is no way to impress a potential boss."

"Maybe you'll find something to wear by then. Try not to worry."

"That's easier said than done."

"I got to get to work. I'll see you later."

"God willing."

Raymond quickly got out of the truck and jumped into his van. By the time he started his engine and was nearly backed out of the driveway, Pookie noticed two one hundred dollar bills lying on the passenger seat. She honked her horn for him to stop.

"Hey… you dropped your money."

"It's your money now. Pay me back with the salary you earn from working at Bettie's."

"But…."

"But nothing," Raymond shouted as he drove away with a huge smile on his face. "You can thank me later."

Pookie gratefully folded and put the money next to her flat bosom in her unwashed bra. She immediately started the truck, for she had decided to go to the nearest thrift store and buy a couple of items to wear before returning to the hospital to visit Shug and June Bug.

When Pookie opened June Bug's door, the first person she saw was Tilly. She was wearing a pair of wrinkled, but clean, green knit pants and a beige blouse. Tilly was not well dressed, but the clothes she was wearing complemented her scruffy brown shoes. Furthermore, her newfound sobriety was the biggest asset she had going for herself.

Shug was sitting next to June Bug's bed. She was surprised when she saw Pookie walk through the door.

"You look so pretty," Shug said, smiling. "I like your black dress and heels."

"You look like a model," Tilly added. "You look so grown-up that no one would believe you're just a teenager."

"Thanks," Pookie said, blushing. "I got an interview with Bettie today."

"Good luck," Shug and Tilly said simultaneously.

"I have some bad news though," Pookie said, looking at Shug.

"If it's about our house being robbed," Shug interrupted, "Tilly already told me."

"I couldn't find Brownie anywhere," Pookie admitted.

"Someone probably stole our puppy," Shug said regrettably. "Let's just hope whoever took him will give him a good home."

"He sure deserves it," Pookie replied.

"Let us know how things go with Bettie," Shug said.

"I sure will," Pookie responded, kissing the comatose June Bug on his forehead before leaving.

The parking lot of the club was full of cars. Pookie could hear the loud music from outside. Lights from a neon sign flashed above the front entrance of the crowded club.

Pookie wanted to just drive away and never return, but she needed the job to financially help Shug. This was not the time to be shy or afraid. Pookie had always dreamed of having this opportunity. She could not let fear stop her.

As she forced herself to get out of the truck and walk across the parking lot, her legs were shaking. She mumbled, "Feet please don't fail me now." It was time for her to go into Bettie's and literally face the music.

Pookie nervously entered the large smoked-filled club. She stood unnoticed among women wearing mini skirts, halter-tops, and stilettos. They sat at tables with their men while the waitress poured booze into their glasses. Some couples were grooving on the dance floor. After noticing the skimpy clothing the women were wearing, Pookie stopped tugging at her modest length dress.

Her nervousness subsided when she saw Toby and Raymond on stage. When the band stopped playing, they came over to talk to her.

"You look beautiful this evening," Raymond said.

"Thanks."

"Let me take you to meet Bettie," Toby said. "These men can't stop looking at you. You're making their old ladies jealous."

Raymond smiled at her and went back on stage. Toby led Pookie by her hand through the crowded room and up a dark stairway to a large suite that overlooked the dance floor. Before Toby knocked on the door, he told Pookie to only respond to Bettie with "yes" or "no" answers and not to say "ma'am" or "sir."

Toby continued to knock before opening the door and walking inside the gaudy room. Two velvet paintings, one of cowboys riding wild horses and the other of dogs playing cards at a poker table, hung on the walls. The carpet was purple and the draperies were red.

Toby told Pookie to have a seat while he went to get Bettie. She sat on the overstuffed fuchsia sofa and waited for them to return. She could not help but notice the unusual furnishings. A wood door was made into a large coffee table, a variety of sweets and Bettie's gold jewelry occupied an antique stand, twin robust armoires stood side by side, and a telephone booth was in the corner.

The very tall and flamboyant Bettie, dressed in white linen pants and leather sandals, then emerged from the back room and sat next to Pookie. All ten of Bettie's fingers had huge diamond rings, which highlighted red fingernails that were so long that they curved.

"You're a cute little thing," Bettie said, almost crushing Pookie against the arm of the sofa. "Are you sure you're ready to entertain the kind of people who come to my club?"

"Well...." Pookie said.

"Well… we'll soon find out," Bettie interrupted. "When can you start?"

"You're hiring me?" Pookie asked.

"If Toby wants you to sing with the band, you're hired. "You just get your act together and be back here tomorrow evening to practice with the guys."

"I hope I don't disappoint y'all."

"So far… no one has," Bettie responded. "Don't you be the first!"

"She'll do just fine," Toby assured.

"Toby… take our newest band member downstairs and introduce her to the guys," Bettie insisted.

"Make sure you and Raymond see to it that she feels welcomed."

"It'll be my pleasure," Toby replied, leading Pookie back down the dark stairs.

Pookie could feel hostility coming from the other band members as Raymond and Toby introduced her. They must have wondered what this young girl could contribute to their already established sound. Pookie knew that she would have to prove herself to them and Bettie as well as to the customers.

To get a good understanding of what she would ultimately face, Pookie decided to stay until closing. She had a lot to think about while she sat, listened to music, and watched patrons dance. After the band covered their instruments and prepared to leave, Toby told Raymond to ensure that Pookie made it home safely. Toby then went upstairs to Bettie's suite where he would be residing for the next couple of nights.

Pookie and Raymond were the only two people left in the club except for an obese security guard and an older gentleman who was cleaning up shot glasses and emptying cigarette-filled ashtrays.

They walked across the empty dance floor, listening to the sound of their own footsteps tapping against the hardwood.

Only Raymond's van, Pookie's truck, and the cars of people too intoxicated to drive themselves home remained in the parking lot. Since it was three o'clock in the morning, Pookie was glad that Raymond was following her home.

Except for an occasional barking dog, Toby's neighborhood was quiet. It nothing like from whence Pookie had moved. There were no thugs standing under the streetlights selling narcotics, no arguing and fighting, or babies crying because their drunkard parents refused to take them home.

Raymond walked Pookie to the porch. He waited for her to unlock the door and go inside. Only when he was certain that she was safe did he prepare to leave.

"Well… now that you're safely inside, I better go."

"Wait, Raymond. Bettie is expecting me to perform with y'all tomorrow night. I don't know what I'm going to sing. I'm going to make a fool of myself!"

"Everything is going to be fine. I know you can sing. I've heard you bring the house down several times with the choir at Mount Holy."

“Please don’t mention Mount Holy when I have to stay here all by myself! It reminds me of Reverend Hurley’s gruesome murder.”

“I’m so sorry. I wasn’t thinking about it that way. To make up for my stupidity, I’ll sit here with you until it’s daylight.”

“I would love that, Raymond.”

Pookie did not telephone Shug to check on June Bug or to share what happened at Bettie’s. If she had, she would have alerted her as to how late she had stayed out. Pookie did not want to worry Shug or give her cause to change her mind about letting her work at the club.

She and Raymond, instead, laughed and chatted for hours until daybreak. Sitting upright, they eventually fell asleep with each of their heads leaning against opposite corners of the sofa.

Pookie was awakened by the noises of children waiting for the school bus. She looked over at Raymond who was still sleeping. For the first time, Pookie saw Raymond differently. He was not the shy, bowlegged boy who sang and played the guitar and drums for her church. He was a handsome gentleman who had stayed the night without once trying to accost her.

She would have liked to show her appreciation by cooking him breakfast, but she did not want to dirty Toby's clean kitchen. Besides, she did not know how to prepare a decent meal outside of oatmeal.

Before going to the hospital to visit June Bug, all Pookie wanted to do was take a bath in a tub filled with warm water and soak until she turned into a prune. She was glad when Raymond finally opened his eyes.

"Was I snoring?"

"No… I didn't hear a peep from you."

"I better get going."

"Thanks for staying with me. I really appreciate it."

"Anytime," Raymond replied, blushing. "See you tonight and don't be late."

After Raymond left, Pookie filled the bathtub with steaming hot water. She found some lavender bath salts on the vanity and poured some in the tub. She sat nude on the edge of the cool cast iron tub as she put her hand inside to make sure the water was not too hot.

The rising heaps of lavender bubbles tickled her

nose. She turned off the faucets and submerged herself into the water. The bath relaxed and soothed her tense body. She closed her eyes and envisioned her and Johnny's one and only sexual experience.

As she began to masturbate, the telephone rang. Pookie wanted to stop the pleasure that was racing through every fiber of her body and answer the telephone. However, the pervasive sensation that captivated her would not permit it.

As she dried off with a plush towel, the phone rang again. Almost slipping on the damp tiled floor, Pookie rushed to answer it. A crying Tilly was on the other end.

"Hello."

"Pookie… it's me, Tilly."

"What's wrong? Why are you crying?"

"Dr. Moss advised Shug to remove June Bug from his life support."

"Why?"

"I think it's because Shug doesn't have insurance. To City Hospital, she's just another poor welfare mother that's taking bed space from potential insured patients."

"What did she decide to do?"

"Shug is taking Dr. Moss' advice. But, she wants you to be with her when she gives June Bug back to the Lord."

"I'll be right down there! Please don't let them do anything until I arrive!"

Pookie then hung up the phone as Tilly was still talking. She quickly got dressed and sped off in her truck. She was driving so fast that she vowed that the police would just have to chase her, because she was not stopping until she reached the hospital.

Once Pookie arrived, she took the elevator up to June Bug's room. Tilly was leaning against a corner with her arms folded while Shug, Dr. Moss, and two nurses were standing around June Bug's bed.

"Are you ready?" Dr. Moss asked Shug as he motioned to his nurses.

"Mama will always love you," Shug whispered in June Bug's ear as she tightly held his large hands and kissed him on his chapped lips. "If there's a God, you'll be among the finest of his angels."

A red-eyed Tilly and a whimpering Pookie watched while Dr. Moss and two nurses disconnected June Bug's life support machine. Within minutes, June Bug took his last breath and his lifeless body conveyed no semblance of the child-like mind that once occupied it.

Dr. Moss gently hugged Shug. He nodded to Pookie and Tilly that it was now over. He and his nurses left the room so Shug and Pookie could be alone with June Bug. Shug asked Tilly, who was also beginning to leave the room, to stay. Tilly knew that if Shug invited her to stay, the past was truly behind them and this was the start of them being friends again.

Shug continued to hold June Bug's hand as she began to talk to his lifeless body.

"I loved you, but God loved you more. Your home is now in heaven. You are forever free of sickness, pain, and unkind people. Meet me at the pearly gates one of these days when my number has also been called. Speak on my behalf when the angels read aloud from my book of deeds to determine my judgment, proclaiming to God that your mother never abandoned you and was your loyal protector until your untimely end."

Tilly walked up to the head of June Bug's bed and

also began to speak.

“June Bug please forgive me for the cruel things I might’ve said when I was drunk. I promise to remain the woman that you once knew and trusted and sought refuge with when life cornered you.”

Pookie wanted to join Shug and Tilly in their testimonies, but her feet turned to stone and were too heavy to move. She just remained standing where she was and sobbed uncontrollably. Pookie watched as Shug and Tilly talked, cried, and prayed over the shell that once housed her jolly brother. From that moment forward, June Bug would only exist in their memories.

As Pookie continued to glare at her brother’s stiff face, she mumbled under her breath. “Where are you June Bug? Where have you really gone? If you are in heaven, will you be retarded there too?” Pookie wanted so desperately for June Bug to answer, but he was not telling.

About twenty minutes later, Dr. Moss returned. A man with gray hair, dressed in a white lab coat, was with him. He did not introduce the man nor did the man acknowledge Shug, Pookie, or Tilly. The man examined June Bug’s body and then immediately left the room.

Dr. Moss handed Shug a long, white envelope. Shug finally let go of June Bug's hand. She took the envelope from Dr. Moss and opened it. It contained funeral arrangements. Unbeknownst to Shug— Toby, Raymond, and Bettie had already agreed that if June Bug died that they would pay for his burial expenses. Dr. Moss said that a hearse from Whitehead Mortuary Funeral Home was on the way to retrieve June Bug's remains.

Eventually three unassuming men came into June Bug's room. They were dressed in black suits, black ties, white shirts, and white gloves. Their black shoes were freshly polished.

One of the men introduced himself as Mr. Tom Whitehead. He attempted to shake Dr. Moss' hand, but Dr. Moss passively declined by putting his hands into his pockets. He then introduced the man to Shug before leaving the room.

While the other two men waited, Mr. Whitehead informed Shug that they were there to remove Mr. James McAdoo's body. He advised that it would be better if she, Pookie, and Tilly waited in the corridor.

Once in the hallway, Shug seemed unusually content. It was as if she was now at peace. Shug thanked Tilly for her support and asked her if she would stay a few days with her and Pookie at Toby's house. With Tammy Sue safe at Mrs. Pearl's home, Tilly gladly accepted.

Pookie then drove Shug and Tilly back to Toby's house. As Shug and Tilly went inside, Pookie checked the mailbox. Scanning through mostly junk mail, she spotted a letter from Johnny. She left the other mail in the mailbox before siting in the swing to read his letter.

My dearest Pookie,

I have had what appears like it's going to be a fast rise to fame in this music business. *My agent has already scheduled me a studio session where I will be recording my first single. I even have some dates arranged to perform at some of the local clubs.*

I will keep you updated on how everything goes. I'm signing off now and will write again when time permits.

Sincerely,

Johnny

When Pookie went into the house, Shug was ironing the wrinkles out of June Bug's blue suit. Tilly was washing his white shirt by hand in the kitchen sink. Shug and Tilly then decided to get some rest, leaving Pookie sitting at the table.

Pookie put her head down and began to cry. She did not know whether she was mourning her brother's death or the fact that throughout Johnny's short letter, he only spoke of himself.

He never once inquired about Shug, June Bug, or even Pookie. Neither did he say he missed or loved her. There was nothing to give Pookie a sign that he still cared. As she wept, she whispered, "Do you still want me to join you, my love? Or has the pursuit of fame formed a wedge between us?"

But just like the questions she had posed to her dead brother, her inquiries went unanswered.

CHAPTER 10

Mrs. Ruth Whitehead greeted Shug, Pookie, and Tilly before inviting them inside. Shug handed Mrs. Whitehead June Bug's clothes. An employee of the funeral home took the clothing downstairs to the morgue.

Shug was then showed six different parlors. Because they all looked alike, Shug just chose the first one she saw. She was then shown the cheap bronze casket that, unless disturbed, would forever be her son's new home.

"What day and time would you like Mr. McAdoo's funeral to take place?" Mrs. Whitehead asked.

"Saturday at two o'clock," Shug replied.

After assuring Shug that that date and time were open, she escorted the three ladies downstairs to the morgue. She wanted Shug to meet Mr. James, the embalmer, and to also inspect the appearance of June Bug's body before it was placed into the casket.

When Mrs. Whitehead introduced Shug to Mr. James, she then returned upstairs. Mr. James did not have to tell Shug where June Bug was located because she immediately saw him the moment they entered the cold room.

Shug walked directly over to June Bug, who was on a metal table. Two other deceased people needing to be embalmed set on nearby tables in zipped body bags.

Except for his shoes, June Bug was dressed in a new gray suit, white shirt, and gray tie. Every string of his thin hair was waxed to lie in place on his large head. Even his bucked-teeth did not protrude from his mouth, which was tightly glued shut.

"Where did these new clothes come from?" Shug asked Mr. James.

"They were donated by the board members of Mount Holy," Mr. James replied, attempting to hand her the blue suit and white shirt in which she had planned to bury him.

"You keep them Mr. James. We'll no longer need them. Maybe another poor family could use them to give their loved one some dignity in death."

Shug then rubbed the tip of her finger across June Bug's waxed mustache. She wanted him to look perfect before asking Pookie for her opinion on his appearance.

With chill bumps covering her arms, Pookie stood over her brother's body. Looking down at him, she thought that he looked more handsome dead than he ever did alive.

While Shug and Pookie continued to view the body, Tilly and Mr. James began to converse.

"Morgues have always given me the creeps," Tilly admitted.

"Well… I got into this business after realizing there's more to fear from the living than the dead," Mr. James replied. "The deceased can't hurt anyone."

"I see your point," Tilly agreed. "Who are the other two deceased individuals? Are they from Alabaster?"

"The one on the left is Mr. Jesse Chappelle. We've been unable to contact a next of kin to claim his body. According to many in the community, he was a recluse that was rarely seen outside his house."

"I'm very aware of Mr. Jesse. He was our neighbor for several years."

"Tomorrow, the state will pay to bury him in a paupers' graveyard, alongside the other unwanted and unclaimed Jane and John Does," Mr. James divulged.

"Who would have guessed that Mr. Jesse and June Bug would end up here together?"

Upon hearing their conversation, Pookie began to think to herself as she slowly drifted closer to Mr. Jesse's body bag. "I didn't tell Shug about Mr. Jesse coming to visit on the day that he died or me going to his house and seeing him with that sissy tramp. If I tell her about him and the sissy tramp, she'll ask too many questions. I can't let her know that I left June Bug at home alone and he became sick after eating that sack of flour." She then had a sudden epiphany. "It was a bag of flour that June Bug ate, wasn't it? Could it have been the missing bag of rat poison that Shug was searching for?"

"Well… what do you think?" Shug asked, interrupting Pookie's thoughts.

"What do I think about what?" Pookie asked with her conscious now riddled with guilt.

"About your brother. Are you satisfied with the way he looks?"

"Yes ma'am. June Bug looks terrific!"

"He sure does," Shug agreed, wiping a single tear from her eye.

* * * * *

Shug, Pookie, and Tilly were the only ones seated in the parlor, except for the three gentlemen officiating June Bug's funeral. The men, wearing black suits and white gloves, had a stoic look on their faces.

Every time the parlor door opened, Shug looked to see who was entering. She was hoping that someone in Alabaster cared enough about her son to attend his funeral.

Reverend Tolliver, the pastor designated to eulogize June Bug, kept coming in and out of the room. He was growing exceedingly anxious for June Bug's funeral to be over because he had two other funerals scheduled afterwards. The family of the next bereaved had begun to congregate in the hallway.

When Reverend Tolliver could not wait any longer he told Shug, in a sympathetic voice, that her time slot was almost over.

Shug told Reverend Tolliver to proceed with June Bug's eulogy. After taking their cue from the reverend, the three men began to close June Bug's casket, but stopped when the parlor door opened. To the elation of Shug, in walked Mrs. Pearl, Priscilla, Portia, Tyrone, Raymond, and Tammie Sue. Raymond was carrying a spray of yellow and white roses. They would be the only flowers to adorn June Bug's grave.

While the new guests made a quick circle around June Bug's remains and said their goodbyes, the three men finally closed the casket and placed the spray on top. Reverend Tolliver began his quick sermon.

As soon as he finished, the three ushers quickly rushed June Bug's casket, family, and friends out of the parlor. They passed the sobbing people in the hallway who were also waiting to eulogize their dead.

After they arrived at the cemetery, June Bug's casket was lowered down into a freshly dug grave. Two gravediggers, in dirt-stained clothes, waited until the mourners left before they began to fill it with piles of unearthed dirt. Shug vowed that she would save enough money to buy June Bug a headstone.

Raymond announced that Bettie and Toby had food waiting for everyone at the club. Although Shug, Mrs. Pearl, Tilly, and Tyrone agreed to go—Portia and Priscilla declined, stating that a club was no place for decent God-fearing folks such as themselves. It was evident that the twins were disappointed that Shug, who had just buried her only son, and Mrs. Pearl, who had buried her husband only a few days earlier, would agree to go to a sinful place like Bettie's. Believing Bettie was a homosexual and thus a disgrace to God, they headed home in a taxi with Tammie Sue.

All, but four, of the clubs' tables were folded and stored behind the stage. Freshly cut flowers atop white linen tablecloths temporarily replaced cigarette burned plastic tablecloths and ashtrays filled with butts. Dinner dishes and an abundance of soul food set on two other tables that were pushed together to make a longer one.

Pookie sat alone on the edge of the stage while Shug and the others chatted and ate for a couple of hours.

"You better eat something," Raymond said as he walked over to Pookie. "You'll need your strength if you're going to work at Bettie's tonight."

"Thanks, but I can't bring myself to eat right now."

"I'll put you a plate to the side just in case you get hungry later."

Carrying two plates of food covered with aluminum foil, Shug came over to where Pookie and Raymond were talking. She wanted to thank Bettie and Toby for their kindness. Raymond told Shug that they were upstairs taking care of some business. Instead of going to interrupt them, Shug decided that she would just thank them later.

She looked over to where Mrs. Pearl, Tilly, and Tyrone were waiting to drive her and Pookie home. Tilly, eager to establish a real mother-daughter relationship with Tammy Sue, notified Shug that she was going home with Mrs. Pearl in lieu of staying another night at Toby's.

"Pookie… when will you start to work?" Shug asked

"If it's alright with you, I want to start next Saturday," Pookie replied.

"That's fine with me," Shug responded. "Pookie… why don't you stay and talk to Raymond? Maybe he can give you a ride home."

"I'll be glad to drive her home," Raymond said.

"Great," Shug said. "I don't want to keep these people waiting. Besides, the car is packed with all of us as it is."

The shy Pookie and even shyer Raymond continued to sit on the edge of the stage long after Shug and the others had left. They were each hoping and waiting for the other to make the first move. Finally, Pookie got the courage to break the silence.

“I want to apologize for my mama putting you on the spot by asking you to drive me home.”

“Don’t apologize. Ever since the day you walked into Mount Holy, I’ve wanted to talk to you.”

“Why didn’t you?”

“Besides you being so much younger, I didn’t think a religious girl like you would talk to a guy who played and sang rhythm and blues.”

“I don’t want to sing religious songs all of my life. That’s why I don’t want to mess up my chances at Bettie’s.”

“Stop worrying. By the way… how’s Johnny doing?”

“How did we get on the subject of Johnny?”

“We haven’t heard from him since he left Bettie’s. Are you two still an item?”

“It depends.”

“On what?”

“I’m not sure.”

“Well… if you need someone to talk to, I’m always here.”

“Thanks, Raymond. That’s sweet of you.”

Toby’s house looked deserted, dark, and lonely when Pookie and Raymond drove up. It seemed to be surrounded with sadness, which reminded Pookie of June Bug. The old red truck, parked on the side of the house, made her long for Johnny.

Pookie wanted to ask Raymond to turn around and drive away, but there was a dim light visible in the kitchen. Shug was probably waiting up for her. This was not the right time for Pookie to take flight and desert Shug. Not on this particular night.

Raymond waited while Pookie checked the mailbox. Inside was another letter from Johnny. As if a strong wind might blow it out of her hands, Pookie tightly clutched it.

Before unlocking the door with the spare key that Shug had left under the mat, Pookie sat in the swing.

Raymond stood on the porch as they conversed.

“Thinking about your brother?”

“And Bettie, too.”

“Why are you thinking about Bettie?”

“I was just wondering if Bettie is a man or a woman?”

“I don’t know, but I’m sure his brother knows and he’s not telling. And neither am I asking.”

“Who’s Bettie’s brother?”

“Toby,” Raymond said as if she should have known.

“I had no idea that Toby was Bettie’s brother.”

“Yeah… he is. They’re planning to move back to France soon.”

“Soon?”

“Don’t worry. You’ll have plenty of time to make your mark. In a little while, you’ll be too big of a star for Bettie’s.”

"Thanks for the confidence. Do you want to come inside?"

"Thanks, but I got to get home and get some much needed rest."

Pookie was glad that Raymond did not accept her invitation. All she wanted to do was go in the kitchen, sit at the table, and read Johnny's letter. Nevertheless, she found herself standing at the door of Johnny's dark bedroom mesmerized by Shug's restless silhouette. Realizing that her mother might need her company, Pookie sat on the foot of her bed.

"I didn't mean to wake you."

"I couldn't sleep, anyway. I was thinking about James," Shug said, calling June Bug by his birth name. "He achieved all a person with his mind could while on this earth. I have to believe that his death is a new beginning for him. He brought what happiness he could to this world and then moved on."

"I agree. Hopefully it's true what they say about time healing all wounds."

"Who's that letter from?"

"Johnny."

"How's Johnny doing?"

"I don't know. I haven't read his letter yet."

"Pookie… this may surprise you, but Toby and I knew each other many years ago before your brother or you were born."

"You did?" Pookie responded, not disclosing that she already knew.

"Well… it's a long story… too long to tell tonight."

"Do share it with me sometime."

"Anyway… Toby called me before you got home."

"What did he have to say?"

"He said that he had something important to ask me."

"And…."

"Patience is a virtue my dear," Shug replied to the inquisitive Pookie. "He said that he and Bettie were planning to return to France and open a new club there."

"Wow… that's nice… I suppose."

"Toby wants me to go with him as his wife."

"As his wife? What did you tell him?"

"He told me to think it over before giving him an answer."

"I don't know what to say," Pookie responded, unsure if her feelings were sadness at the prospect of her mother leaving, jealousy that she was unable to be with Johnny, or anger that she had stayed behind to help Shug only now to be abandoned.

"But don't you worry, Annie Lee McAdoo," Shug said, also calling Pookie by her government name. "I'm not going anywhere until I'm sure you'll be fine without me. Heck… you can come with us if you like."

"If you don't want to leave with Toby, you don't have too. Johnny will soon be very successful and he'll take care of you and me."

"That's what worries me!"

"What worries you?"

"I don't want you waiting on a man to take care of

you! What happened to your dreams of becoming a successful singer on your own?"

"I still have those dreams."

"Then achieve them so you can take care of yourself! You can begin at Bettie's!"

"I suppose you're right."

"We'll talk more about this tomorrow. Are you coming to bed?"

"Later. I'm going in the kitchen to read my letter."

"Goodnight. I'll see you in the morning."

"Mama…."

"What?"

"Who's Bettie?"

"Bettie is the person who hired you."

"I meant… is Bettie a woman or a man?"

"Bettie is a kind-hearted person and that's all that matters. Always pay attention to a person's actions and not their words. And look at what's in their hearts instead of their outer appearance. That way you'll avoid wolves in sheep's clothing."

CHAPTER 11

The first few weekends of singing at Bettie's were disastrous for Pookie. Some of the club's regular customers booed and ignored her. Pookie would have quit and abandoned any dreams of superstardom if she had not taken some much-needed advice from Raymond. He suggested that she pretend she was singing in church. He thought this would help her because church is where she had been most comfortable. Raymond said that Pookie should pretend that the patrons were the same people she used to see at church on Sundays. Heeding his words of wisdom, Pookie eventually began to gain fans among the clubbers that had once shunned her.

It was not long before she was belting out such soulful songs that everyone in the smoke-filled club stopped their laughter and loud conversations, giving their undivided attention. Word quickly spread around Alabaster and surrounding towns about the young, skinny girl with a golden voice. As new people began to frequent the already overcrowded establishment, Pookie's salary increased. This afforded her an opportunity to also increase the money she gave to Shug.

After work, during the wee hours of the morning,

Pookie would often write letters to Johnny. She shared her small steps toward fame with him. Besides telling him how much she loved and missed him, Pookie also expressed how proud she was of him and the recent success he had achieved by signing his first major record deal. It would be a matter of months before he would be shooting his official video to complement his single.

Although Pookie's letters were steadily increasing, Johnny's letters were becoming fewer and fewer. When he did write, he only talked about himself. For just once, Pookie wanted to read a letter about how proud he was of her. She wanted him to confirm if he still loved her and proclaim that he could not wait until they were together again. But to Pookie's dismay, she interpreted none of those signals from him.

Pookie began to believe that Shug's words of wisdom were correct. Maybe she should depend on herself and not on Johnny. Pookie was ashamed to tell Shug that she rarely heard from him. Out of embarrassment, she would pretend that everything between her and Johnny had remained the same. Pookie would sit at the kitchen table and read the same old letters over and over, pretending to Shug as though they were new ones.

On one particular Saturday after Bettie's closed,

Pookie shared the lie she was living with Toby. As the band members unplugged and stored their instruments, Pookie and Toby sat on the edge of the stage and talked.

"Shug and I are getting really close," Toby said. "If you know what I mean."

"I know what you mean," Pookie said, smiling.

"Raymond would be a good man for you. Why don't you give him a chance?"

"What about Johnny? Is he a good man for me?"

"Johnny is a good man for someone, but not for you."

"I wish Johnny would write or call me more often or at least come to visit sometime?"

"Fame is a hell of a drug. I've seen it change the humblest of people."

"I never want to change."

"Well… when you become rich and famous, remember the ones who supported and loved you."

"Don't worry. I don't think I'll ever get that famous."

"I'm going to tell you a little secret. Some music scouts will be at the club tomorrow night. They're interesting in hearing you sing."

"Why didn't you tell me earlier so I could prepare?"

"I just did. Besides… they like to keep their presence a secret."

"Wow! I guess that's good news."

"It's fantastic news. You need to really impress them because they can take you places you've only dreamed of!"

"I'll be sure to give it all I've got."

"Shug won't agree to marry or leave for France with me because she doesn't want to abandon you."

"I'll always need my mother, but I want her to be happy, too."

"She certainly deserves some happiness, so get your act together. I know you can do it!"

"Thanks for the encouragement, Toby."

"Don't forget Raymond. He's also pulling for you… even if your success means he might lose you."

"I didn't know he cared so much."

"Raymond loves you unconditionally. And unconditional love, my dear, is hard to find."

On the night that the scouts were coming to the club, Pookie was more anxious than her first night ever singing at Bettie's. However, she was well aware that this might be her one and only chance to prove that she was made for show business.

People occupied every table and chair. There were patrons standing on the dance floor and at the bar due to the large crowds there to hear Pookie sing. Even Shug, Tilly, Mrs. Pearl, and Tyrone were in attendance. They sat at a table reserved for Shug and her guests.

Raymond brought Pookie a glass of water to soothe her dry throat. When the band began to play, the audience became quiet as she slowly walked to the microphone. Tightly grasping the microphone, Pookie sang her heart out. Even the range that her voice reached surprised her.

During the break, a man came over and introduced himself as Mr. Kenneth Wilkerson. He said that he was a talent scout and that he would like to speak with her privately. While he and Pookie went upstairs to Bettie's suite, Shug and her party of three anxiously waited.

When Pookie returned to their table, she had a big smile on her face.

"Spit it out," Shug said with her hands to her cheeks.

"What did he say?" Tilly asked.

"Mr. Wilkerson wants to manage me," an excited Pookie said.

"I knew you had it in you," Shug responded.

"We are so proud of you," Mrs. Pearl and Tyrone added.

Pookie had within a week to decide if she wanted to sign a contract with Mr. Wilkerson's management company. However, her only thought was sharing it with the guy she loved, Johnny Overtree. She surmised that that was just enough time for her to surprise Johnny by visiting him in Chicago. She felt it was essential to talk face-to-face with him before making her decision. She would take the northern bound train to do just that.

It was at that moment that Pookie realized that there was so much more for her to see and achieve beyond Alabaster. She wanted to travel and have many exciting adventures in both music and her life. Her dream of becoming a professional blues singer seemed to be unfolding. Nevertheless, as always, her thoughts got the best of her. "With whom will I share my success? I want so much for it to be Johnny, but what about Raymond? If Toby was right about him loving me unconditionally, who then should I give my heart to?"

* * * * *

After the train arrived at the Chicago Union Station, Pookie collected her luggage before hailing a taxicab. She took one of Johnny's letters from her purse, reading the address aloud to the cabby. He weaved in and out of the congested traffic.

"Are you talking to me?"

"Of course I'm talking to you! You're the only one in my cab. Where are you coming from?"

"Alabaster, Georgia."

"Is that where all the bastards are born?"

"I wouldn't know."

“I was just kidding. If you’re thinking about living here, in Chicago, you better grow some thicker skin.”

“I’m just visiting. I came to surprise my boyfriend.”

“When it comes to girls surprising their men, the surprise is usually on them.”

When the taxi finally arrived at Johnny’s address, Pookie gave the driver three twenty-dollar bills. She then waited for her change of ten dollars. Upon setting Pookie’s bags on the curb, the once friendly taxi driver called her cheap before speeding away.

Pookie was impressed with the two-story brownstone buildings and their windows filled with boxes of pansies. The small lawns were mowed and surrounded by white iron fences.

Carrying her luggage, Pookie entered a building with five zero one posted above the entrance. The lounge was neat and clean. Although the worn carpet was vacuumed, there was a faint, yet musty odor in the air. The sofa and chair cushions sagged where many derrieres had sat. Pookie went to the receptionist and spoke to a woman who was reading a newspaper.

“May I help you?”

"Yes. I'm looking for apartment seven… where Mr. Johnny Overtree resides."

"It's upstairs on the right."

"Thank you."

"And tell Mr. Overtree to try to keep the noise down."

Pookie could hear the sounds of people talking and laughing in Johnny's apartment. Before she could knock, a shirtless man, dressed in tight black pants, opened the door. Four beautiful, voluptuous, young women followed behind him as he headed toward the stairs. They passed by Pookie as if she were invisible. She was somewhat envious of the females who were clothed in tiny shorts, tank tops, and stilettos. Pookie's constant stares forced the man to turn and speak.

"Whatever you're selling, Miss, we aren't buying."

Johnny, who was still wet from just showering, suddenly appeared at the door. His damp body caused his red briefs to cling to his body. Water from his freshly shampooed hair dripped onto his well-developed hairy chest. Pookie's legs began to tremble at the sight of him. Johnny was even more handsome than she had remembered.

Realizing that it was Pookie, Johnny called out to the man who had mistaken her for a salesperson.

"Hey, Kross! Come and get this luggage and take it to my bedroom."

"Anything for you boss," the man replied, humiliated that Johnny had ordered him around in front of the four women.

Johnny then kissed Pookie on her cheek and escorted her inside to the sofa. On the coffee table were ashtrays with squashed cigarettes, empty beer bottles, and soda cans. Johnny had to push newspapers to the side so she could have a place to sit.

"Why didn't you tell me that you were coming?"

"I thought I would surprise you."

"You sure did."

"How are you, Johnny?"

"Since I left Alabaster, a lot of good things have happened for me. My musical career has taken off like a rocket!"

"Mine, also. That's the main reason I'm here. I want to know where we stand as a couple."

"Let's continue this conversation when I come back. Kross is driving me downtown to the studio for a very important recording session. Make yourself comfortable and we'll catch up when I get back."

When Johnny left, Pookie made sure his front door was locked. She then went into his small cluttered bedroom to unwind from the long journey. Expensive jewelry covered the dresser and the drawers overflowed with fancy underwear. Johnny's closet was bulging with designer clothes. Pookie surmised, "Wow! He wasn't lying about things changing. Would he even want a country girl like myself now that he's been around these city girls?"

Exhausted and confused by Johnny's lack of excitement at her presence, Pookie took a bath, got dressed in a new pink nightgown that she had purchased to impress him, and then went to bed. She was awakened, hours later, by the sound of Johnny talking and laughing with some other people in the living room. She looked at the clock, which displayed three o'clock in the morning.

Without checking to see if Pookie was awake or if she wanted to join their fun, Johnny closed his bedroom door. For two hours, Pookie listened, contemplating if she should pretend to be asleep or not, as Johnny and his guests partied into the wee hours of the morning.

After the last person had left, Johnny finally came into the bedroom. He undressed and got in bed next to her. Johnny wrapped his warm nude body around Pookie and gently kissed her on the nape of her neck.

Although he smelled of old cigarette smoke and stale beer, Pookie was eager to make love to him. However, within seconds, he had begun to snore. Unable to sleep, Pookie went into the kitchen and sat on a stool at the bar. She tried to think, but her mind was blank.

After approximately an hour had passed, Johnny also came into the kitchen. Wearing only his briefs, he poured himself a glass of orange juice and drank every drop before taking the glass from his mouth.

Pookie followed his every move. Her body ached for his affection. Pookie was more mature and she now wanted him the way he had wanted her when they were in Toby's bathroom. It was obvious that on this particular morning that she would have to be the aggressor.

Pushing her shyness aside, Pookie went and stood behind Johnny as he set his glass on the counter. She pressed her body against his broad, muscular back. She slowly moved her hands down his hairy chest toward his pubic hair and penis. Just when

Pookie thought she felt something rising from inside his briefs, Johnny moved away from her and sat on a stool. Pookie felt like a complete fool as she glanced at her cheap-looking gown, which made her feel more like an old grandmother than a vibrant young lady.

"How long are you planning to stay?"

"It depends on you."

"What does that mean?"

"Johnny, have your feelings for me changed?"

"Pookie…."

"Please tell me the truth."

"I didn't mean for things to change between you and me. They just did."

"Would you like for me to leave?"

"That might be best. It's a busy time for me now."

"So, where does that leave you and me as far as our relationship or plans for the future?"

"I think we should give it a couple of years and see how things go," Johnny said, obviously having moved on from any and all things Alabaster, including Pookie.

"Okay," Pookie said, determined not to let him see her cry.

"I have an appointment downtown this morning. I'll be gone for about five hours. Will you be here when I get back?"

"I don't know, yet."

"Well… make sure to tell everyone that I send my regards."

"Johnny…."

"Pookie… please try to understand. I'm in a different place in my life right now."

"But, I…."

"Look… if you're still here when I come back, I'll see you safely to the train station."

Johnny then went into his bathroom to shower. Pookie was heartbroken. She was so low that she considered losing the last of her respect and dignity like the once intoxicated Tilly had done with those two men.

As she listened to the water coming from his bathroom, instead Pookie quickly changed into the same clothes she had traveled in. She grabbed her luggage and hurried out of the apartment and down the stairs. When Pookie passed the receptionist, the woman's face displayed a look of sympathy for her. She nodded at the naïve Pookie as if to say, "This too shall pass."

Once outside, Pookie flagged down the first taxi she saw. She sat in the backseat, sobbing with her face enclosed in her hands.

The train ride back to Alabaster seemed shorter than she would have liked. Pookie wanted it to keep going and going for she was not yet ready to face the reality of what had transpired in Chicago. Neither did she want to admit to anyone, especially Shug and Toby, that she and Johnny were no longer the couple she assumed they would always be. Once the doors to the train opened, she had no choice but to EXIT.

All she desired was to slip into Toby's house and lick her wounds in private. However, when she stepped onto the platform, Raymond was waiting with a big smile on his face and a rose in his hand.

"Tired?"

"Yes, but I'm not ready to go to the house."

"Where do you want to go?"

"Just drive anywhere."

"You got it!"

"Thanks for being my friend."

"I'd like to be more than your friend… if you'd let me."

"Raymond… I decided to sign that contract with Mr. Wilkerson and I don't ever want to return to Alabaster. I'm going to give Shug and Toby my blessings so they can marry and move to France."

"I understand, Pookie."

"I don't think you do Raymond," Pookie said, feeling somewhere in between loneliness at losing the love of her life and attraction to Raymond's loyalty and devotion. "I can't ask you to leave your home and go with me, but…."

"You won't have to. Since Bettie's closing… Mr. Kent hired the band to travel along with you. Would you mind if we tagged along?"

"Not at all!"

"Will you marry me, Pookie? Let's make a life together, vowing always to be a refuge for one another in this cruel, cruel world!"

CHAPTER 12

It was not long after Shug and Toby married and moved to France that Pookie and her band, Raymond's Rhythm Riders, began selling out concerts. Within seven years of signing her management deal, she was one of the biggest names alongside Aretha Franklin, Gladys Knight, and Patti LaBelle.

Except for Johnny and Pookie's music occupying the Billboard Hot 100 Chart and receiving roughly the same amount of radio play, their paths never crossed again—not even within the small circles of the entertainment industry.

Bettie and Toby's new French club, Open Doors, had also become very popular. To celebrate their tremendous success, Toby and Bettie invited Pookie to guest perform there. For five consecutive weekends—Pookie and Raymond's Rhythm Riders headlined the club.

During the weekdays, Pookie and Shug spent every moment with each other. They shopped for hours in quaint boutiques, dined on Pot-au-feu, visited the Eiffel Tower, took long walks in the park, and drank afternoon tea at some of the finest outdoor cafés.

Shug talked nonstop about how much she loved Toby while Pookie confessed that she had fallen in love with Raymond.

"Has Raymond asked you to marry him?"

"Several times. I always tell him to give me more time to think. It's been years now and I guess I'm still thinking."

"If I were you, I'd go right now and tell him that you'll marry him. Raymond has proven that he loves you… for who you are… and not the image of perfection the world has formed of you from watching you perform on stage."

Pookie took her mother's advice. During their last performance in France, Pookie and Raymond were married inside of Open Doors. Their union was on the cover of most magazines and constantly repeated on news programs. It was one of Pookie's happiest moments. However, as always, tragedy was lurking somewhere closely behind.

Six months later, Shug and Toby died in a car accident. Pookie and Raymond returned to France to attend their funeral.

Pookie paid for a specially made double casket so they could be laid to rest side-by-side. Shug was dressed in a paisley green silk dress and pearl earrings. Her attire complemented Toby's green suit, white silk shirt, and paisley green tie.

Bettie, wearing a lavender dress and canary yellow heels, and Pookie, wearing a black designer dress and hat with a veil, walked slowly around the bronze casket as they viewed the bodies.

"Are you pleased with the funeral arrangements?" Bettie asked.

"Very much so," Pookie responded. "But, why did you chose the color green for their attire?"

"Green is the sign of spring and new beginnings," Bettie replied. "Hopefully, even in death, there's a new beginning for Toby and Shug."

"You do everything with such class," Raymond said. "Pookie has on green panties, too."

"I do, too," Bettie said, laughing.

Two black Arabian horses pulled Shug and Toby's hearse up a grassy knoll. Raymond lagged behind Pookie and Bettie as they walked beside the hearse. Shug and Toby were buried in the French countryside under a large spreading oak tree, facing pastures where cows roamed and grazed.

As Bettie and Raymond began to descend the hill, Pookie stayed behind to say her last goodbyes.

"Who would have thought that this day would come, my dear mother? Your words of wisdom and knowledge have led me through this life of mine. I cannot thank you enough for always believing in me and being my biggest cheerleader. Upon June Bug's death, you claimed that if God is willing that you'd see each other again. Well… if there is a heaven, I want you and June Bug to meet me at the gate when it's my time. My dearest Toby, I remember what your nephew, Johnny, once said to me. He said that you might become my best friend and he was so right."

With a heavy heart, Pookie proceeded down the knoll. The thought of Shug, June Bug, and Toby, resting eternally together, however, consoled her.

Pookie then heard the familiar tune of a distant train. She smiled and pondered, "Maybe Shug and Toby's souls are on that train, traveling off into the far distance." She watched the slow locomotive glide along its track until it rounded the bend and was out of sight.

The train's rhythmic sounds and melancholy cries brought back many memories and unanswered questions.

Pookie remembered the Roberson's and wondered how they were and if they were still alive. She thought of the Hurley's and especially Alspice and Mrs. Pearl. She wondered who murdered Reverend Hurley.

The death of Mr. Jesse then came rushing into her mind. She contemplated if he had really perished in his house fire or if it was actually the sissy tramp, allowing him to leave town while concealing the murder of his wife, Mrs. Ruby. Pookie hoped that Tilly was still living a sober and happy life with her teenaged daughter, Tammy Sue.

She pondered if Bettie was really a man or a woman and if, now that Shug and Toby were deceased, they would ever see each other again.

She then thought of Brownie, wondering whatever became of him, and if a caring family adopted him. Her final thoughts were of Johnny and whether he ever thought of her or if he regretted the way he had treated her when she came to visit him in Chicago.

But, it was too late to discover the answers to those questions. That was the past and as it stood, the only way Pookie could relive it was in her mind. Knowing some truths could be a burden too heavy for her derriere to carry. She would have to forever wonder.

Raymond left Bettie, who continued to walk behind the hearse, and came back up the hill to be with Pookie. She affectionately squeezed her husband's hand as they strolled down the path together.

Before Pookie and Raymond boarded their airplane back to the states, Bettie handed her an envelope and a jewelry box that belonged to mother. On the flight home, Pookie read Shug's letter.

Dearest Annie "Pookie" Lee,

If you are reading this, it means that God has called my number. I wrote this letter when Toby and I first moved to France and gave it to Bettie for safekeeping in the event something ever happened to me.

I want you to have my special jewelry that my beloved husband gave me. Wear and enjoy each piece as I once did. If lost or stolen, don't cry. They're only material things, anyway. But always protect the greatest gift anyone can give you and that is unconditional love.

Raymond loves you unconditionally. He will protect and shelter you as I have. I am so proud of the woman that you have become. Stay true to your humble beginnings and never allow fame to change the little girl in you with the golden voice that got her start singing gospel.

I will be watching over you until we meet again.

Love Always,

Mom

CHAPTER 13
(CONTINUED FROM CHAPTER 1)

Early on Sunday morning, Mabel and Jed returned to work a day before scheduled. They wanted to survey the premises to ensure that the house was safe and secure. As they entered through the garage, they were surprised to see Lee's car for they assumed she would still be out of town.

Mabel told Jed that Lee must have changed her mind about taking a trip down south or perhaps, she had returned earlier than expected and was upstairs in her bedroom. That is when they found Lee, lying unconscious at the bottom of the stairs.

"Mrs. Lee!" Mabel screamed, "Are you hurt?"

"Where am I?" Lee asked, dazed.

"You're at home," Mabel responded, helping Lee to sit up.

"What happened?" Lee asked.

"You must've fallen down the stairs and hit your head," Jed answered. "Luckily your luggage buffered your fall."

"I told you not to forget to eat," Mabel said, going into the kitchen to get some orange juice.

"Thank goodness we had to come back today," Jed added.

"What time is it?" Lee asked.

"Eight-thirty in the morning," Jed responded, looking at his watch.

"Sunday morning?" Lee asked.

"Yes, ma'am," Jed answered.

"Do you want us to call the doctor?" Mabel asked, forcing Lee to drink a glass of orange juice.

"No… that won't be necessary," Lee responded. "I guess it was all just a dream."

"What was?" Mabel asked.

"Oh, nothing," Lee replied. "I'm just thinking out loud."

"Are you sure you don't need a doctor?" Jed inquired.

"No… I'm fine," Lee responded, preparing to go upstairs. "Mabel will you bring me something to eat to my bedroom, please?"

"Right away," Mabel replied. "Do you want me to unpack your luggage?"

"Store my luggage in the downstairs closet," Lee said. "They'll be already packed for my trip to Europe to be with my husband."

"What about your trip down south?" Mabel asked as she went into the kitchen to cook her some food. "Isn't someone expecting you?"

"Jed… Mabel," Lee said, pausing at the top of the stairs, "some skeletons are best left in the closet to crumble."

As Lee proceeded to her room, she mumbled, "Sister… I thought of a name for your book." She then smiled and whispered, "Let's call it EXIT."

WE HOPE YOU ENJOYED READING *EXIT*....

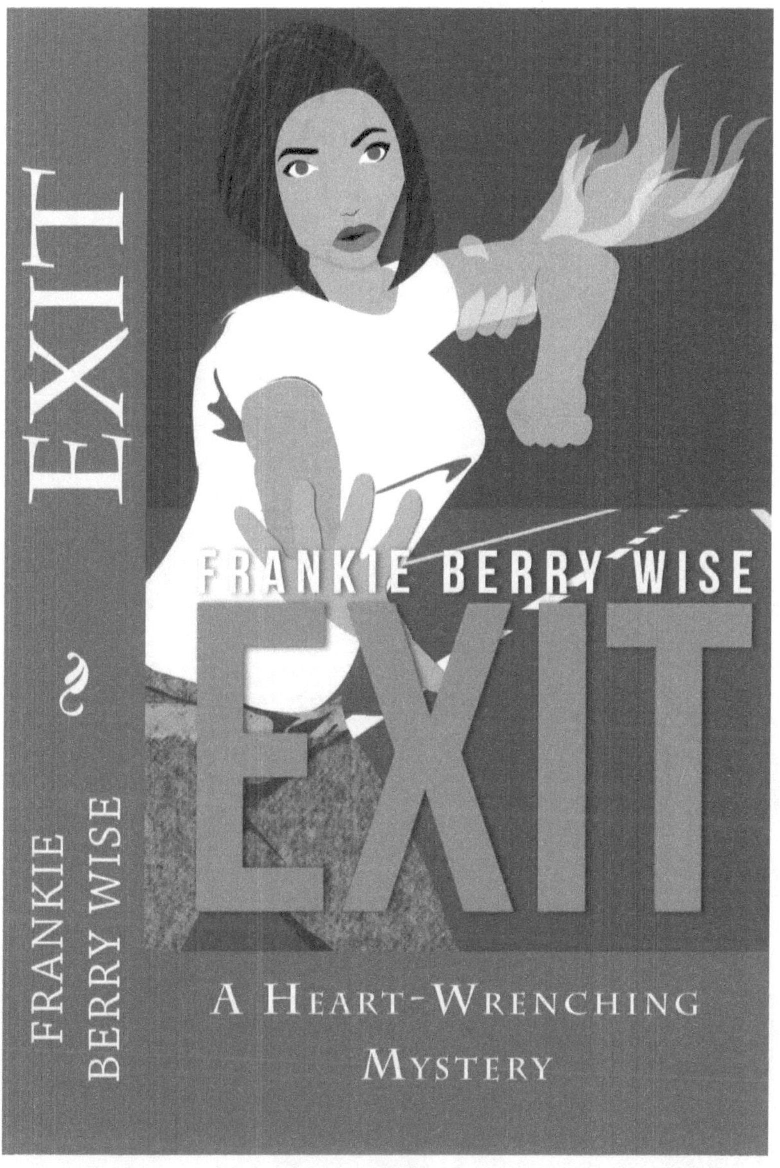

Turn the pages to learn more about some of our other publications and literary selections!

WISE
SCHOLARS PUBLISHING
We Bring LIFE to LEARNING

Available in Paperback, Hardback, and E-Book

BREAKING THE CHAIN

FRANKIE BERRY WISE

CONTACT US

www.wisescholarspublishing.com

www.facebook.com/wisescholarspublishing

wisescholarspublishing

@marshalettewise

marshalette@wisescholarspublishing.com

1-888-735-6392

1-334-452-4596 (Fax)

www.ingramcontent.com/pod-product-compliance
Lightning Source LLC
Chambersburg PA
CBHW030355310726
48979CB00001B/311
* 9 7 8 0 9 9 6 3 9 4 6 2 8 *